A DYING FALL

A DYING FALL

•

Laura Shea

AVALON BOOKS
NEW YORK

Published by Thomas Bouregy & Co., Inc.
160 Madison Avenue, New York, NY 10016

Library of Congress Cataloging-in-Publication Data

Shea, Laura.
    A dying fall / Laura Shea.
        p.   cm.
    ISBN 0-8034-9809-8 (acid-free paper)   1. College teachers—
Fiction.   I. Title.

    PS3619.H45D95 2006
    813'.6—dc22

                                                    2006018081

PRINTED IN THE UNITED STATES OF AMERICA
ON ACID-FREE PAPER
BY HADDON CRAFTSMEN, BLOOMSBURG, PENNSYLVANIA

I wish to thank the following people: Laureen Griffin, Deborah Williams, my sister Sally Sweeney, Karen Galatz, and Tom Doherty. Without your enthusiastic support and encouragement, this manuscript might never have seen the light of day.

And to my colleagues over the years, none of whom teaches at Brixton University, I wish to express my gratitude for all I have learned from you. Thank you.

Chapter One

A little more than kin and less than kind.
–William Shakespeare, *Hamlet*

It looked like the kind of place co-conspirators would spend their time until they found God or a better lawyer. Though some might beg to differ, it was not a prison but a place of higher learning. Brixton University stood on the site of the exploded brickworks and was built, it seemed, from the remains of the day when the town's main export showered down upon a startled group of workers who quickly fled the scene. Brixton took its name from the pile of rubble left behind by the brickworkers and its style from their handiwork. Over the years, a number of architects had continued to favor brick for the low-slung buildings and high-rise towers, the brownstone and the Bauhaus dotting the campus. The result was a mix of then and now that was hard to place on the architectural map.

Brixton University was founded a century ago to minister to the needs of the community, with preachers and teachers a specialty. It now served a different clientele: those who do their father's work because no one else will hire them. Separated by a river and several million in endowments from its nearest neighbor, a school favoring old ivy and older money, Brixton was at the top of the class among the second tier. The sun would always shine on the school across the river, but Brixton stood firmly in its shadow, accepting this position along with all major credit cards. The two universities eyed each other warily.

On a day in late fall, when the poet's thoughts turn to dying, a determined band of professors enjoyed their last meal at the river. At the end of the hour, or fifty minutes by the academic clock, they would return to the duty of teaching a thing or two to the youth in their charge.

"Erica Duncan, child of scorn."

"Oh, I think I know this one," said Erica. "What is "Miniver Cheevy," by Edwin Arlington Robinson?"

"That's where it's from, and that's what you are. And this is not an episode of *Jeopardy*."

"Don't be so sure," Erica said to her colleague, Sarah Tillney. "I just wanted to know which literary theory currently reigns supreme, and I knew you would know."

"Where is this sudden urge coming from?" asked Sarah.

"Well," said Erica, "I might be trapped in the elevator with one of our more venerable scholars and forced to make conversation. I don't want to seem too out of it."

"Just a little out of it," Sarah ventured.

"Just enough to fit in."

"Erica, you may pretend to ignore the scholarly debates in the English Department, or to be above the fray, but you work among people whose livelihood depends on such things. You must have absorbed something in the process."

"Yes, and like second-hand smoke, it's probably harmful to my health," Erica replied. "I know you've got to have a gimmick—I mean, a theory—to guide your every thought. It certainly makes things easier in the publish-or-perish scheme of things if you can adapt your thinking to the current theory of choice. It's just so hard to keep up. What do you do when a work of literature does not conform to theory? Ignore the evidence? Look the other way?"

As she spoke, Erica reached into her brown bag, found an orange, and started peeling.

"All the fields of literary study begin to sound like Polonius' categories. You know, in *Hamlet*, when Polonius announces that the actors have arrived, 'the best actors in the world, either for tragedy, comedy, history, pastoral, pastoral-comical, historical-pastoral, tragical-historical, tragical-comical-historical-pastoral,'" Erica said in a singsong voice.

"Of course I do," said Sarah with a little sniff.

"Well, it's a short hop to talking about new critical, historical, new historical, phemonenological, psychoanalytic, sociological, sociological-historical," said Erica in one breath.

"That's enough, Erica."

"No, I have more," said Erica. She took a breath and continued her list. "Marxist, sociological-Marxist, archetypal—"

"Please stop," said Sarah, slightly pleading.

"Structuralist, semiotic, structuralist-semiotic—shall I go on?"

"No," said Sarah firmly.

"And Polonius was mocked as a figure of fun," said Erica.

"So will you if you share this with anyone else in the department," Sarah replied.

"No chance of that," Erica admitted. "We don't share much beyond the weather and the wait at the copy machine. Anyway, I've been trying to lay low until the next critical revolution," she continued, "waiting for the next set of operative phrases. Little did I know that the word *post* can be slapped in front of anything, and we're stuck with it for another twenty years."

"Well, there's feminism, of course; that will hold you in good stead," Sarah said.

"It's done wonders for me so far."

"Fine, be that way," said Sarah, taking a long look into her own brown bag before retrieving half a turkey sandwich. "But explain to me, in light of your critical vacuum, how you managed to get hired in the first place?"

"Well, there's the wit, the charm, and the red hair."

"Keep going," said Sarah, as she fingered a stray lock that a colorist might identify as flat brown.

"You must know this," said Erica. "It's a favorite among bedtime stories."

"I was on leave, remember?"

"Oh, yes," said Erica, "The fancy fellowship across the river. I heard about you."

"And I, you," said Sarah. "When I returned, there you were. Though the reason why has escaped me."

"Someone died, of course," Erica said, neatly spitting out seeds between syllables. "You remember, Professor Landesman. The one who dropped dead on Labor Day weekend over a year ago."

Erica paused for a moment to contemplate the flight

of time and to dispose of the remainder of her lunch, squashing the seed-laden bag in her hand. "Anyway, I was in the right or the wrong place, and the rest is history."

"They didn't grill you on literary theory at the interview?" Sarah asked.

"The only thing they were interested in grilling were the hamburgers on the barbeque heating up at home," said Erica. "It was an emergency. They needed a warm body, preferably able to teach. They did ask at the interview if I had theory, and I said no, just lots of practice."

"Heh heh heh," said Sarah, in a deliberately stilted manner.

"That's exactly what they said. No wonder you do so well around here," Erica said.

"Anyway, I got the job. I later discovered that my answer had a high approval rating when several members of the hiring committee assimilated it and made it their own."

"They stole your line?" Sarah asked, looking genuinely surprised.

"Borrowed it without benefit of footnotes," said Erica. "Really, they are welcome to it."

"We know there's more where that came from," said Sarah.

"We like to think so. As to the big theory question: I try to avoid any curriculum that avoids contact with the actual literature. So, I just teach the plays. Nothing fancy, just the thing itself. The students seem to like it. I think it makes a nice change for them. They are a little tired of studying literary criticism instead of literature, not unlike eating the cook and leaving the stew."

"I will overlook the veiled comparison of critical study

to cannibalism," Sarah said. "We can debate the merits of criticism another time." She lifted her face to the sun that gently warmed them. "This weather is wonderful."

"Enjoy it now," Erica said. "It won't last."

"If you don't like New England weather, wait a minute," said Sarah.

"Who was it who said that?" asked Erica. "Mark Twain? Al Roker?"

"All of the above," answered Sarah. With a quick glance at her wristwatch, she asked, "What's on your schedule for the rest of the afternoon?"

"The usual, only worse," Erica sighed. "Student conferences highlighted by the visit of a plagiarist."

"*Alleged* plagiarist," said Sarah.

"Of course," said Erica. "Innocent until proven guilty—and this kid's bright enough to do the work himself—but he copied someone else's and got caught. For some strange reason, plagiarism absolutely infuriates me. It's lying, cheating, and stealing all at once—"

"A triple threat—"

"The original sin as far as this profession is concerned. Those who do come up with something new usually don't break the mold, they just scrape it away."

"Now, now," said Sarah, in her placating way.

"I have to admit that, despite my strong feelings on the subject, I am a bit squeamish at the prospect of facing the little cheat," Erica continued. "I mean, I've got a guaranteed conviction—xeroxed proof in my hot little hand—but how to broach the subject? 'Oh, by the way, you're going to fail my course, but (lucky you) you won't be thrown out of school, because I have neither the time nor the inclination to take you before the Honor Council.' "

Sarah nodded. "I don't blame you. Remember what

happened to the fellow who mishandled that plagiarism case last year. As I heard it, he forgot to make a copy of the paper in question—"

"—which the student conveniently lost, along with all memory of ever having written it—"

"All the student could remember was the phone number of her parents' lawyer. Then they got up in front of the Honor Council, it came down to one word against another, and the teacher found himself on trial," finished Sarah.

"What would they charge him with?" asked Erica. "Doing his job?"

"I don't know the technicalities," Sarah answered. "The student's stance was 'I am not a plagiarist.' Anyone who got in the way of that was guilty of something, as far as daddy's lawyer was concerned. As I recall, the whole thing ended in a draw, but it was messy all around."

After her long speech, Sarah revived herself with a sip from her water bottle.

"Whatever happened to the professor?" Sarah asked. "I haven't seen him lately."

"That's because he left," answered Erica. "Got another job."

"Where?" Sarah asked.

"I don't know," Erica answered. "And what *was* his name?"

Sarah thought for a minute. "Honestly, I don't recall."

"Me neither," said Erica. "Not very collegial of us."

"Demerits all around," said Sarah. "He didn't leave because of the cheating incident, I hope."

"He wasn't the one who cheated," replied Erica. "No, I don't think that's what led to his departure, and it's not like we own the franchise on plagiarists," she said as she checked her watch. "With that encouraging anecdote in mind, I don't suppose you'd like to make a guest appearance during my office hours and speak to the alleged offender? Good practice, you know."

"No, thank you," was Sarah's measured response. "Just repeat what you said to me, especially the part about lying, cheating, and stealing, and he'll be begging for mercy. I know I nearly was." Sarah neatly finished the last bite of her sandwich before continuing. "How did you know the work was plagiarized? If the student did a halfway competent job—"

"Oh, yes. He probably got through high school copying term papers out of the encyclopedia."

"Or off the internet," said Sarah. "Somehow, I can't imagine you poring over article after article, just because you had a feeling that a student had, shall we say, appropriated the work of another. You'd figure out some non-commital way of accusing him and bluff it out. How did you know?"

"For the best of all possible reasons," said Erica slowly, speaking over the chimes of the angelus telling them it was time to go. "Pure coincidence. I was at the dentist last week, waiting for my turn in the chair, grading papers as usual. I graded and I waited until I got sick of both and started looking through the antiquated selection of magazines in the waiting room— *Newsweek*, for one. It wasn't last week's or last month's, and it wasn't recent enough to be found just anywhere. I flipped through the magazine and stopped at one of the essays on the nature of man, or something equally ambitious—you know, full of lively writing, topical allusions, and too hip for its own good. What did I see?

An uncut version of the student paper I had read not half an hour before. Isn't that amazing?"

"Indeed. Where would we be without the long arm of coincidence?" Sarah asked.

"What do you mean 'we,' *kimo sabe*?"

"Actually, I meant literature," said Sarah. "We'd certainly miss those neat endings, the last minute rescue—"

"The stunning revelation: 'No, you cannot marry him. He is your brother.' Where is a deus ex machina when you need one?" Erica wanted to know, as they gathered their possessions and prepared to go. "The long arm of coincidence," she added, "I hope it strangles this kid."

"Now, now," said Sarah, "the last time I checked, death was not the penalty for plagiarism."

"Maybe it should be," said Erica.

"Moving on," Sarah quickly countered, "Will you be making an appearance at the event this afternoon?"

"You mean my yearly opportunity to have a drink at the expense of the English Department?"

"That's the one."

"Of course I'll be there," said Erica. "Only death, disaster, or something better to do would keep me away."

"Good. I'll see you there," said Sarah. "You might want to be early—"

"I thought society arrived late."

"I'm sure it does," Sarah began.

"But *they* don't," Erica finished. "Academics take everything very seriously, up to and including their drinking."

"But that's what you love about them," Sarah said.

"Let's just leave it at that," said Erica. "Better yet, let's just leave."

Chapter Two

For what's a play without a woman in it?
–Thomas Kyd, *The Spanish Tragedy*

Only in America, thought Erica, *only in the land of the free and the home of the brave can the condemned man provide his own stay of execution.* Upon returning to the Department, Erica found in her mailbox a small square of pink paper, meticulously filled out by an anonymous secretary, informing her that the alleged offender had telephoned while she was out and couldn't make his appointment, for reasons too complicated or indelicate to fit on a small square of pink paper. Erica crumpled the note and muttered a faint expletive.

Leaving the mailroom, she passed the centralized perch of Letticia Franklin, the chief secretary, the one who managed management. Letticia's vaulted position precluded her from leaving phone messages but not from knowing what they said. Letticia could barely contain a squeal of girlish glee—no mean feat for a more-than-middle-aged lady—and would not have hidden her satisfaction for all the privileged information in Departmentdom.

"Little voices are telling me that you are less than pleased," Letticia said.

"That's funny," said Erica. "My voices tell me to go and save France."

A quick intake of breath was Letticia's only reply. Erica walked away, knowing that her mail would be late and her phone messages sporadic for the next few months.

With the cancellation of the alleged plagiarist, Erica had some time before the arrival of her office-hour regulars, a select few who came without appointment or apparent purpose other than to find someone to talk to, or at, as the case may be. The poet Robert Browning said that we should lend our minds out; Erica had found that an ear was usually enough. Her students rarely came seeking answers. All they wanted was someone who listened, nodded at appropriate intervals, and occasionally offered a suggestion. She tried to keep the customers satisfied.

Erica's officemate was out teaching a class, which left her to contemplate a view of the fire escape in unabridged privacy. Her mind wandered to a regular haunt, to the question of what she was doing here. The road less traveled, as usual, made all the difference.

Erica had come to Brixton as a graduate student. In a unique form of earn as you learn, graduate students, as practice professors, teach what they can to those who can't. For Erica, that meant writing, in English, if possible. For this she received a salary rivaling that of a moderately successful match seller. After a while, this arrangement offered her two options: living up to her previous financial obligations (an undergraduate loan had come calling) or living up to her present financial obligations, which included eating. Before the love of literature ruined her life completely, a detour into a more lucrative profession was called for—a move encouraged by the lending institution that followed her career with interest and enthusiasm.

A fine education had honed Erica's ability to turn a phrase on demand and to sound sincere while doing it, especially on topics about which she knew little and cared less. Clearly, the ad game was for her. Before long, she had written her way into copywriting history as the anonymous coiner of the phrase "My wash is everything to me." (Yes, that was hers.) Apparently, enough people felt that cleanliness was underrated where godliness was concerned, and sales of a certain detergent increased dramatically. Erica could have stayed on Madison Avenue, creating the American way of life, but there was unfinished business in academia, where leaving is not that unusual, though coming back is almost unheard of—unless you're in need of a quiet place to wait out a statute of limitations.

With money in the bank, Erica returned to finish her doctoral degree—the terminal degree, as it is known. She emerged from her hiding place in the library, the site of a frenzied few months of dissertation writing, to collect her diploma and to announce her imminent departure, rather than face the worst academic job market since the twelfth century. The fortuitous passing of Landesman (she was sure he was in a better place) left a space to be filled by the time the vans pulling up to the curb were unpacked.

Brixton rarely hired its own, for academe tries to marry up, hiring people with degrees from schools more prestigious than the one paying the salary. But this was an emergency. As the exception that proves the rule, Erica was willing to ignore the show of no confidence if the department was willing to add a year to the standard one-year contract. Viewing contract negotiations as strictly a spectator sport, the hiring committee was surprised by her demand but agreed, rather than spend the weekend, or the rest of the afternoon, finding someone else. So there she was, with only herself to congratulate or to blame.

Erica roused herself and turned to the most recent pile of undergraduate offerings, the kind sometimes better burnt. Personal narrative was a fixture of the course that she was required to teach and they were required to take. Her students might but slenderly know themselves, but they had a lot to say on the subject. She plunged into the stack before losing her nerve. The first paper began: "You know that commercial that says, 'This pasta will last longer than most marriages?' My parents just passed their expiration date." *Cute,* thought Erica. *Why are you telling me this?* Let's try another.

"Emmett had eleven fathers," the next paper read. She chose not to read on. She looked up to find the first of the usual suspects waiting outside her open door, for once standing on ceremony by preparing to knock. Grateful for the interruption, she welcomed him. The doctor was in.

Chapter Three

If they ever make a cannibal stew of you,
Invite me too . . .
–Cole Porter, *Anything Goes*

Erica had grown up in an era when writers made it perfectly clear that no man is an island unto himself. She had dutifully taught the literature of isolation to not-yet-alienated and hardly self-sufficient freshmen. To her belief about requisite togetherness she would add that the more disparate the parts, the tighter the whole and the hold they had over each other. Standing in the Founder's Room at the English Department's annual cocktail party, surrounded by the about-to-be's, one or two now-and-ever-shall-be's, the been's, and the never-had-been's (was there a pluperfect tense for failure?), Erica watched them prove her rule. The group could explicate the ways of the ancients, but when faced with each other, they were stumped. "Equality" had once been the cry of the day, and though all were overeducated, underpaid, and in need of a drink, they had managed to go beyond race, class, gender, and certainly beyond sex (it was all metaphorical anyway) to a place where having nothing in common provided the social glue. Erica's fascination with this curious paradox was hardly morbid. Like the rest, she knew there was a job to be done. 'Twas the season to be rehired, so, armed with an indifferent chardonnay, she prepared to give and take on the gossip market, savoring the disembodied comments that floated around her, wondering what or who was on the block today.

"The baby is very expressive," Erica heard a proud father say. She edged in the opposite direction, having hit the snooze button on her own biological alarm clock. The merits of parenting could wait, especially after a recent conversation with a new mother who had announced that the baby's name was "MacKenzi, with no *e*."

"None at all?" Erica had asked.

The conversation had ended so quickly that Erica was not sure whether the child was a boy or a girl.

"Open admissions are an open admission of a death wish for the university," a male voice stated in a tone that had seen little use since the death of Churchill. Realizing that this was the wrong corner of the room, and unwilling to turn around lest she recognize the speaker, Erica was weighing the risks of sidestepping her way across a crowded room when a familiar voice confided: "Someone told him at an impressionable age that he had a way with words. They failed to mention that it was the wrong way."

Erica turned to find Jamison Bordwell, barely controlling his impersonation of an aesthete-in-waiting.

Bordwell was making his critical name by dragging from obscurity a late-nineteenth century poet who spent most of his life in his library. There, the poet had imaginary conversations with wise and famous men, letting the servants do the living and, presumably, the cleaning up afterward. Born about a hundred years too late, Jamie, as he was known to all, was doing what he could with the fin de siècle that he had. The mode of decadence he espoused was a fairly tame variety, suitable to his tenured circumstances.

"I was just about to bolt," said Erica, happy to come upon someone who could wring professional advancement out of any occasion.

"You can't leave yet," Jamie said. "The ablutions have just started, and after hors d'oeuvres, we shall exorcise an evil spirit or two. You don't want to miss the ritual sacrifice."

"Anyone we know?"

"To be named later. Suggestions are being accepted after I get another drink. Can I bring you something?"

"I'm fine, thanks."

"Yes, you are."

Erica smiled as Jamie skillfully made his way to the bar, and quietly blessed the luck of the draw in matching her with so suitable an officemate. Not long after his return, the nearness of alcohol and each other rubbed out certain transitions, and the pair spoke in a conversational shorthand, noticing things that couldn't possibly be missed, at least by them.

"I didn't think he'd be here," said Jamie.

"Who?"

"O'Brien. He who was betrayed."

"Oh, yes," said Erica. "From golden boy to goat in a matter of days."

"A matter of minutes was more like it," said Jamie, almost to himself.

"I know that tenure meetings are a deep, dark secret, Jamie, but what could they possibly object to in O'Brien? He did it all. He taught, he published, he slaved, he served. What did they find to hold against him? Outstanding parking tickets?"

"A little knowledge can be a dangerous thing, Erica. Just remember that for some of our colleagues, holding grudges is their only form of exercise. O'Brien's tenure case was a chance to flex those muscles. It really had nothing to do with him—"

"It's only his life," Erica hastily pointed out, "and after they kick him to the curb, it's not like he can scamper off to a new job next week or next month. Academic jobs roll around once a year, unless there's some kind of an emergency. *Maybe* there'll be a position in his field, and *maybe* if he went to the right schools, people would be willing to talk to him—but the negative tenure review makes him damaged goods. He's not unhireable, but not as desirable as he might have been."

"All too true," Jamie admitted. "Unfortunately, there was nothing he could do or have done, for that matter. A member of the senior faculty decided to remind a few people of favors past due, and the rest of us, of his existence. For reasons as yet unknown, he scuttled O'Brien—just because."

"I don't mean to sound naive, but who would do such a thing?" asked Erica.

"One who beggars description," Jamie answered with barely muted disgust. "It's probably best to avoid our angry young man, at least for now. His case is not closed, and I don't think he plans to go quietly."

"This could get interesting. We all know what a man scorned can be like."

"Do we?" asked Jamie.

Seemingly on cue, Larry O'Brien chose that moment to make his way across the room. His usual swagger was slowed a little by the number of people in his path and the quantity of alcohol and humiliation he had recently partaken. Larry came to rest in the vicinity of Jamie. His gait may have been unsteady, but his gaze was level as he looked into Jamie's face and said with a grin, "I'm going to kill that bastard." Then, he moved on.

"Anyone I know?" Erica inquired.

"Let it be, Erica. The man had a little too much to drink, that's all." They observed a moment of silence for the soon-to-be-departed O'Brien, while Erica scanned the room.

"Do you know him?" she asked, certain of the an-swer. "The one striking the Byronic pose, over there by the window."

Jamie looked in that direction. "Moronic, did you say?"

"Byronic, and you heard me."

"Pieterese, isn't it?" Jamie asked, though it wasn't re-ally a question. Among the potential chairmen, which in-cluded his rival by the window, Jamie was certainly a contender. Erica knew that Jamie considered Raymond Pieterese a mere pretender to the throne. Currently keep-ing the chairman's seat warm was Curtis Greenspan, whose professional interests centered on the early retirement package he was negotiating with the administration. This left his surrogate children to fight it out for the place that their papa gladly relinquished.

"Our friend Raymond invited me to visit his class once."

"What a treat for you," said Jamie.

"I think the plan was to dazzle me with his style—teaching and otherwise. Do you know that he strikes that same pose in class? He looks winsomely out the window, waiting for inspiration to strike."

"Which it does, regularly," said Jamie. "Like a gong."

" 'Now, now,' as Sarah would say." Erica briefly wondered why Sarah wasn't there, saying it herself.

"Friend Raymond gave a wonderful class. At least, that's what he told me. 'I really had them' were his exact words. If the students agreed with him, they were had, all right. To the untutored eye, Raymond seemed to be free-associating his way through a whole lot of literature."

"And did you reciprocate, Erica? Invite him to your place—I mean, class—to exchange pedagogical stances?"

"No," Erica replied. "I think the idea was for me to be impressed—*very* impressed. I had my chance and I blew it." She shrugged. "Oh well."

The smoke in the room, not quite taboo, was beginning to envelop them, aided and abetted by one particular pipe.

"Leventhal seems to be sending us smoke signals," Erica observed.

"He's sending signals," Jamie said, "but I don't think they're intended for us."

One of the odder couples to be found at any departmental gathering was the pairing of Professors Leventhal and Grayson-Grossman. No one knew which came first—the Grayson or the Grossman—either way, Leventhal was sure to follow.

"From what I know of her, she is as impeccable as her credentials," Erica said. "Not to mention, married and completely unavailable. In other words, no chance."

"Erica, it's *supposed* to be unrequited. Anything else would be too scary—for him, anyway. She would manage quite nicely, I expect."

Erica looked at the two of them: Natalie, graciously accepting whatever benefit his homage and senior status might bestow upon her, and Stewart, behind her, puffing away. The little engine that couldn't.

"And he's not married, right?" said Erica, finding the level of frustration in the room, like the smoke, hard to tolerate.

"Not to my knowledge. Are you looking, Erica?"

"Oh, no," she replied. "I wouldn't want to get in the middle of that." She followed Jamie's gaze in another direction.

"Now that man has panache," she began.

"A word rarely heard."

"Fewer know what it means."

"But Gorman—"

"Agreed."

In a world of publish or perish, Mark Gorman had done neither and survived in style. One might question his scholarship—if there were any evidence of it—or quibble with his habit of marinating himself in musk—but his ability to parlay a small amount of charm and a sympathetic ear into a full professorship impressed even his detractors. His name did appear in print, adorning trucks, signs, and the cardboard backing in shirts. "Gormanizing" had revolutionized the dry-cleaning business. His family had dirtied its hands in trade so that he would not have to, but woe to the neophyte that made the connection and mentioned it. At least one overeager assistant professor now rode the tenure track in a place where conversations focused on the price of corn and the height of horses, or perhaps the reverse.

Rumor had it that Gorman was one of a dying breed, those who teach without need of salary, a dollar-a-year man. If true, the price was just about right. At one time, Gorman had taught a survey course in Shakespeare, his field of expertise, until a number of undergraduates found it difficult to be in the same room with him. Jamie had taken over the course and returned it to its previous luster and enrollment. Gorman now taught the odd seminar to the small number of graduate students who should have known better than to sign up. Erica thought it best to keep her distance until fate or promotion evened the level of their stations.

Jamie and Erica watched the parade go by. They saw those who knew that biology was destiny, and those who knew better. And here and there, the person as intelligent and ambitious as the rest, but with the added element of humanity, who taught by her own example—Elizabeth Lane, known as Elaine, for reasons no one could remember, was one such exception. For far too long the only tenured women in these parts—an oversight remedied with the help of a federal judge— Elaine was an eminent Victorian who made her name when there was still something to say about Tennyson.

A certain local notoriety had resulted from Elaine's habit of rescuing stray dogs. In the past, she had been known to give five dollars to a cab driver who would take a hungry-looking mongrel to the nearest fast-food place for a quick cheeseburger on the way to the animal shelter. Nowadays the dogs were not as lucky. Too much sidewalk space was taken up by humans in need of a break today, and they received her largesse, minus the cab ride. The poverty line had to be drawn somewhere. Elaine's philanthropy was no pretense, unlike her pose as an amiable eccentric, which camouflaged a mind that charted the zeitgeist before it was in the air. When she repeated the latest item, it went from gossip to fact before she finished the sentence.

"Enjoying the punch and cookies, are we?" Elaine asked, surveying her younger colleagues.

"Trying, Elaine, trying," Jamie said. "Will you join us?"

"I wish I had seen you sooner," she answered, making her way toward them. "It would have made for a pleasanter time. My husband is here somewhere, waving madly the last time I saw him, before he was swallowed by the mob. He loathes these events, not to mention a few of my colleagues. It's a wonder he's even willing to pick me up, but I had to promise to be ready and waiting by the door, having answered the call of duty, nature, and anything else by the time he got here. I forgot to include travel time—mine, not his. It takes forever to get across a crowded room, did you know that?"

"I plan to leave the next time I get near a door—or window," said Erica.

"I'd offer to drop you somewhere, but I anticipate marital discord on the way home. He must be ready to kill me."

"Before you go, Elaine, at least give us the latest bit of vital information," Erica said, "and only if it's none of our business."

"If you insist," said Elaine. "Beware the ides of March and Professor Parkinson. I don't know why, but he's behaving very strangely. He's *smiling*. Now, I really must be off."

With the ides a distant future (it was late October), Elaine's departure left them considering Professor Parkinson, who stood not far from them, inevitably alone. He did seem to be favoring the world with an odd facial expression. In his case, what passed for a smile was more of a crumpled line creasing his face.

"The merry medievalist," said Jamie.

"He knows something," Erica said in ominous tones. "Tell me, have you done anything that he wouldn't do?"

"I beg your pardon, Erica," Jamie returned, "there is nothing he wouldn't do—and he's looking at you."

Erica looked in Parkinson's direction, managing to avoid eye contact. Jamie was right, though she had no idea why Parkinson would favor her with his attention. His twisted grin reminded Erica of a nursery rhyme she had not remembered since childhood.

> *There was a crooked man*
> *Who had a crooked smile*
> *Lived in a crooked house*
> *And ran a crooked mile.*

"I'm not brave enough to know what's on his mind. I think I'll leave before there's any chance of finding out," Erica said.

"I'm ready to go," said Jamie. "Shall I be cavalier enough to escort you to the nearest form of public transport?"

"And they say chivalry is dead," Erica answered.

"I didn't promise you my seat."

The pair began to make their way through the milling crowd, stopping at the cloakroom to retrieve briefcases and coats. When they finally reached the door, Erica took a last look around the room, wondering what had become of Sarah. Parkinson was still offering a strange expression to no one in particular, like the cat that not only swallowed the canary, but savored the fact that it went down alive.

What is he thinking? Erica asked herself. Of more immediate concern was the question of why people converge at doorways. In trying to step out into the street, she was greeted abruptly by her colleague John Crandall, who, upon entering the room with his usual grace (head down, feet first), managed to scatter Erica's possessions on the floor around them. Following in his wake was his wife, Tish, who at least had the good grace to look embarrassed.

"Well, John, I was hoping to bump into you," Erica said as she retrieved her briefcase. "Tish," she nodded.

"Oh, Erica, well, I—excuse me," John mumbled as he stepped by her and quickly made his way into the room. Tish hesitated for a moment, torn between two automatic gestures: to follow her husband, or to pick up after him. Sensing her dilemma, Erica waved her away. Tish proffered a grateful smile, turned, and trotted after him.

"And they say that chivalry is dead," Jamie laughed, as the two freed themselves from the tangle at the doorway, bracing for the weather that, true to Erica's prediction, had turned cold.

"Dead and buried," said Erica. "Dead and buried."

Chapter Four

I like a look of agony
Because I know it's true—
Men do not sham convulsion,
Nor simulate a throe—
The eyes glaze once—and that is Death—
Impossible to feign . . .
–Emily Dickinson

Parkinson died that afternoon. He was found in his office by a janitor emptying the wastebaskets that were never filled, and the ashtrays into which no one flicked anything. If he had been planning to die, the way he went about it was slapdash at best. A dictionary dropped on his head, and out, out, brief candle. It was his favorite, the monumental *Oxford English Dictionary,* which fell from the stand beside his desk and cracked his skull, among other things. How does a man lean so far back in his chair that he manages to upend a dictionary? No one seemed to know. What can you say

26

about the man who died? Especially one who introduced himself as "Parkinson—like the disease." That is
a little easier to answer: He was pedantic beyond the
call of duty. He was the type who kept to himself because everyone left him alone. He caught a dictionary
right between the eyes.

Few of his colleagues subscribed to the sentimental
belief that the dead become more likeable because they
are dead, though at least a dozen said that nothing in his
life became him like the leaving of it. (To live a life
without allusion would be unthinkable.) Parkinson was
in death what he was in life, only quieter about it. His
presence had been noted by the relentless clatter of the
manual typewriter behind his office door as he tried to
make the world safer for Chaucer. He had, he used to
say, a medieval mind, and rarely faced an age-old question without finding an age-old answer.

In death, he seemed to have found something more.
Almost before the blood on his carpet was dry, there
was talk of Parkinson's latest, and last, published effort. It had something to do with whips and chains and
The Wife of Bath's Tale, an approach to Chaucer by
way of the Marquis de Sade. Before long, Parkinson's
critical coup, known as the new sadism, was taking
hold of the collective imagination. The sadists set about
gauging the threshold of pain in a literary work by asking the critical question: How much does it hurt? This
question was applicable to all genres and generations
of literature, just the ticket if creative forms of degrada-
tion got your interest. It appealed to a number of scholars who had very nearly deconstructed themselves into
oblivion. The hastily named neo-Sades gave as good as
they got, searching for pain and inflicting more in the

process, the thing seen and the seer inextricably mixed. It seemed unlikely that Parkinson had intended to found a school of criticism, but there it was. All in all, a touching tribute to the man who died.

Chapter Five

When I think of life I think I mean more than anything
else the beautiful show of it, in its freshness, made by
young persons of your age. So go on as you are.
  –Henry James, *The Ambassadors*

"**D**id you hear?"

"How could I not? It was a little hard to miss the police cruiser double-parked in front of the building."

"Well, that's nothing new. There used to be regular
visits to a former colleague, the vice chairman, a title
which turned out to be apt. Before your time."

"Would you save that little piece of history, Jamie?
One shocking revelation per day is enough."

"It will have to wait in any case. I have a class to
teach. On my way back, I plan to offer solace to our
own Letticia, who seems to be taking this very hard. I
will dry her tears and she will tell all," said Jamie.

Passing her that morning, Erica had seen the re-
doubtable and very married Letticia, dabbing her eyes

with a lace-edged handkerchief in a show of real distress at the abrupt end of Parkinson. Erica was not privy to the twists and turns of Departmental alliances over the years, but she hadn't expected this to be one of them. Strange bedfellows indeed.

Erica dismissed this thought with a mild shudder, turning her attention to the couple that stood in the doorway recently vacated by Jamie. Robin Reynolds and Ned Lowery were among the best and the brightest of Brixton's current crop of graduate students. Robin was as voluble as Ned was silent. In his first three months of matriculation, Ned had not uttered a single word, and people began to wonder if a pre-verbal candidate had managed to slip undetected into the graduate program. Letticia Franklin had broken at least one silence in confirming his perfect scores on the entrance exams. Robin then took the situation in hand, finding that Ned responded well to direct questioning. For the most part, Robin still did the talking, translating his thoughts and hers, leaving little doubt as to what was on their mind. They seated themselves on either side of Erica's desk, and Robin began, seemingly mid-monologue:

"I can't believe he's dead. We were in his Chaucer class, you know. It was truly awful. I mean, I know you're not supposed to speak ill of the dead, but it was the worst. On the first day, he told a roomful of graduate students that reading *The Canterbury Tales* was like packing the station wagon and driving cross country."

"He said *what*?" asked Erica.

"I know, great way to teach Chaucer," Robin continued. "I mean, if we were twelve or something. Right, Ned?"

Robin leaned in to Erica as she confided in a stage

whisper, "Ned's parents used to take him on trips during the summer. He refused to get out of the car in forty-eight states." Robin smiled at Ned, who nodded. *That explains a lot*, thought Erica. She moved the conversation in another direction.

"Did Parkinson have a wife, a family?"

Robin and Ned shrugged in unison.

"Did he have a first name?"

"He was always just Parkinson to us," said Robin. "Or Professor to his face."

Or worse behind his back, said Erica to herself. "Come on," she said. "Students always know everything, graduate students especially. What's the word on the investigation?"

"The what?"

"The investigation. Are they dusting for prints?"

"Prints?" asked Robin, looking puzzled. "In case you haven't noticed, they don't dust for dust around this place. As far as I know, the police came, they saw, they're calling it an accident." Robin looked to Ned for confirmation on this point, which he offered with another nod. "Not easy, but an accident," Robin finished.

That a dictionary had served as lethal weapon was old news by this time. More than a few weighty tomes had been moved to safer locations. In other rooms, recreations were being staged, with side-splitting hilarity, if not head-splitting results.

"You're really getting into this, aren't you?" Robin asked, intrigued. "Were you, like, friends or something?"

"Friends? I barely knew the man," Erica said quickly. "I just thought an investigation was what happened when someone dies under, shall we say, unusual circumstances."

"Too much television," said Robin. Ned nodded in agreement.

"You may be right," said Erica. "With something like this, we expect it to look like every cop show we've ever seen—or like the news, film at eleven, yellow tape across the door of the crime scene."

"Chalk marks of the victim's body on the floor," Robin said.

"Blood stain on the rug." Erica and Robin quickly looked at Ned, who had offered this insight.

"I peeked," he said.

"Anything else?" asked Robin in a rising tone.

"No prints. The police looked, just in case."

"The place was wiped clean?" Erica asked.

"You really *are* into this," said Robin with surprise.

"No, there were too many prints," Ned said. "Parkinson's office was covered with prints and with dust, the kind that the police didn't put there. It only makes sense that it would be harder to dust for prints in a dusty place."

Thank you, Dr. Watson, thought Erica.

"I'm not sure I want to know how you know all this," Robin said. The long speech seemed to have exhausted his resources, and Ned returned to shrugging as his primary means of communication.

"And what prints are you talking about?" Robin asked Erica. "What are you suggesting?"

"Not a thing," Erica said. "It seems that Parkinson did this the same way he did most things—alone. I'm just indulging some morbid curiosity, that's all—at Parkinson's expense, it seems."

"I know something you don't know," said Robin in a singsong voice.

"Don't keep us in suspense," said Erica.

"Well," said Robin, leaning in conspiratorially. "I was in the little girls' room this morning, and heard a couple of the secretaries talking. You may have noticed that Letticia hasn't turned off the waterworks since they found Parkinson."

"It has been noted."

"Well, it seems that she's all choked up because he dedicated his last article to her."

"Why would he do that?" asked Erica.

"Beats me," Robin answered. She began to sing. " 'This is dedicated to the one I love.' "

"That's a bit of a stretch," said Erica. "Maybe he was just being nice."

"That's a bigger stretch," said Robin.

Erica decided to try a different tack. She said to Robin, "I'll bet you read *Nancy Drew* books when you were little."

"Didn't everyone?" answered Robin.

"Nancy has been discovered by women's studies," said Erica.

"A feisty feminist in her jaunty roadster?" asked Robin.

"Something like that," Erica replied. "I read the most marvelous quote a while ago from the original author—the books were written by a franchise after a while. Anyway, the one who started it all had lived in peaceful anonymity, counting her royalties, until the new Nancy-mania. She said something to the effect of 'I'm so sick of Nancy Drew, I could vomit.' "

"Sounds like a feisty old girl," said Robin.

"Now we know where Nancy gets it," said Erica.

As they talked, Erica noticed Sarah moving quickly

down the hall with the slightest hesitation as she passed Erica's open door. It was not unlike Sarah to rush around, given the quality of her life. A Renaissance woman, Sarah managed a career, a husband, and two children, the ten-year-old twins, Philip and Sidney. Sarah had what is commonly known as 'it all.' If Erica lived Sarah's life, she would simply have had it. But it was unlike Sarah not to stop and acknowledge them, even in passing.

Ned, on whom the moment was not lost, turned to Robin and said, "Next shift." As they got up to leave, Robin asked, "Any chance that you'll take over the Chaucer class? We've already done the preliminary work, packing the station wagon and everything. You could pick up where Parkinson left off."

"I was the last hired, so I'm undoubtedly the first to be exploited," Erica replied, "but I think that honor is intended for someone else. Besides, it's not my field—not even close."

"Too bad," said Ned. Erica considered this high praise indeed.

"Yeah," continued Robin. "Parkinson was making us read everything, and I mean every, last, boring word he ever wrote about Chaucer. Here it is." Robin reached into her backpack, extricated a stapled sheaf of paper, and dropped it on Erica's desk.

"Nothing like a captive audience," said Erica.

"Yeah," said Robin. "A long, hard look at the collected mediocrity of Parkinson." Ned and Erica looked at Robin.

"Well, it's true, isn't it? I'm not enough of a hypocrite to pretend that's changed, just 'cause he's dead.

It was a killer career move, though." Ned and Erica again looked startled by her comment.

"I mean, dead artists get more for their work, don't they?" Robin asked. "What about dead academics? Does this up the price on Parkinson's stuff?"

"Academics usually don't make a lot of money on their publications," Erica tactfully explained. "At least not the type of thing Parkinson did."

"I get it," said Robin, nodding. "Worth every penny."

Chapter Six

"Very well, Lady Teazle, I see you can be a little severe."
–Richard Brinsley Sheridan, *The School for Scandal*

Erica caught up with her friend in the mailroom. They seemed to be alone but, as in *Hamlet*, eavesdroppers could be anywhere. Erica quietly asked, "Do you have a minute? In my office?"

"Fine," Sarah said quickly. They walked together, speaking only after Erica had closed her office door.

"A closed-door discussion?" Sarah began. "What's up?"

"What's up" was so far from Sarah's usual style of communication that Erica knew immediately that things were not right in the Sarah universe. Erica decided to tread carefully, saying, "We missed you at the party. Did something come up?"

"Yes."

"Nothing serious, I hope."

Sarah did not answer.

"Okay, are we going to play twenty questions or are you going to tell me?" So much for Erica's diplomatic skills. "I can see that something's wrong," she added, more gently.

"I hope that I am not as painfully transparent to everyone," Sarah answered. "Yes, I skipped the party. I was not in a party mood."

"Why not?"

"Perhaps it was childish of me . . ."

"Sarah, you are a model of restraint. When I grow up, I want to be just like you."

"I thought we were the same age."

"I'm a late bloomer. So what happened?"

Sarah let out a sigh before answering. "After I taught my afternoon class, I came back to check my mail, and I found a copy of a teaching evaluation completed a few weeks before by a member of the senior faculty. It's standard practice—the kind of thing you can look forward to when they put you on the tenure track—"

"*If* they put me on the tenure track."

"We'll see. In any case, I found the evaluation very disturbing. Not that I consider myself above reproach—"

"Though you are—"

"But this report was so completely critical, so vicious and destructive, that I cannot see what purpose it could possibly serve. I shall spare you the gory details, but if what he wrote is in any way true, I should be banned from the classroom for life."

"You are a wonderful teacher. We all know that. Even the students know that," said Erica.

Sarah went on. "Do you know that this *person* sent me a memo over a month ago announcing his visit. He never appeared, so I thought the visit would be rescheduled. Then he popped into my class one day, without a word of warning. Of course, he has the right to do that—"

"But it's very rude—"

"Worse than that, unprofessional." Sarah was finally allowing herself to be angry. "And he was disruptive once he got there. He made his presence felt by sitting in front where all the students could see him, and shifting in his seat for the duration of the class. If a student behaved that way, I would reprimand him or her, but with a senior colleague, who should certainly know better . . ."

"No," said Erica. "You can't." For the moment it seemed better not to offer lengthy comments, but to wait until Sarah had run out of steam.

"Not only was I infuriated by the way he behaved, but now I have no opportunity to question the evaluation. These things do make a difference, you know."

Erica nodded, confident that Sarah's ducks would be back in a nice, neat row in no time. Sarah was about to continue, when Erica stopped.

"Wait a minute, why can't you challenge this? You have that right, at least."

"He's dead."

"*Parkinson* did this?"

"Yes."

"That would complicate things."

"Yes," said Sarah again, with more emphasis. "I had the inestimable pleasure of being savaged by someone who is—who was—a notoriously bad teacher."

"So they say—and apparently, a real slime into the bargain."

"Well, he did me one favor by trying to head butt that dictionary."

Aha, thought Erica, *a soccer mom.*

"If he were alive, I'd feel obligated to smile and exchange pleasantries when we met, and then spend my free time thinking of a way to kill him. Now that he's dead, that's one less thing for me to think about."

"Good of him to be so considerate," said Erica.

"Goodness has nothing to do with it," said Sarah.

Erica could only nod.

Chapter Seven

In matters of grave importance, style, not sincerity, is
the vital thing.
–Oscar Wilde, *The Importance of Being Earnest*

Parkinson's passing generated some discussion in the
Department with little sustained interest. But a death is
a death, and if it bleeds, it leads, so a member of the administration was called upon to mouth the appropriate
clichés to the local media, offering a virtually unrecog-
nizable portrait of Parkinson as teacher, scholar, and
all-around saint. *Brixtonia,* the student newspaper, offered a black-bordered blurb with an oblique reference
to the "unfortunate accident" that had taken the teacher
from his students. Their lack of interest was not sur-
prising, given that it was Homecoming Week, which
most of them took literally. Ignoring the campus festivities, most of the students went home.

After a decent interval, a memorial service was
planned, in keeping with the brand of secular human-

ism peculiar to academics. The deceased had practiced a form of Christianity more appropriate to the author he adored, favoring a spirited mingling of the sacred and the profane. Parkinson's remains were unseen at the service, which was fine with Erica, never a fan of life-like corpses and with little fondness for the ubiquitous urn. Someone had chosen a reading from the Parkinsonian canon, a mercifully brief disquisition on *The Consolation of Philosophy*, proving once again that a little Boethius goes a long way. Erica wondered if it were doing Parkinson any good now, if he was well and truly consoled—no one else seemed to be.

At the sparsely attended event, held in the same room that housed the Departmental cocktail party, Erica wondered whether the funeral baked meats would resemble last week's hors d'oeuvres, though refreshments were not yet in evidence. *Definitely a no-frills affair,* thought Erica, as she tuned out a eulogy even briefer than the Boethius, spoken by Curtis Greenspan. His pained manner telegraphed his sincere desire to be just about anywhere else. *Though not where Parkinson is,* Erica mused, still uncertain of the exact location of the deceased. She had heard something about cremation (the urn again) and wondered where the ashes would be tossed, and possibly, in whose face. The accessories of death are there for the living, after all.

Ever the teacher, she took attendance and found more than a few people notable by their absence. Then again, in light of what she was learning of Parkinson's popularity, this was a sellout crowd. Sarah had decided to pass on this event, as had John Crandall. Natalie Grayson-Grossman had chosen to attend, and Stewart Leventhal would be where she was, though neither looked too happy about it. Elaine and Jamie were there. Raymond Pieterese's Byronic pose certainly worked in this setting. It looked like someone had forgotten to tell Mark Gorman and Larry O'Brien that attendance was not mandatory. The two sat in the back row, glowering together.

Erica was surprised to learn of the existence of Parkinson's wife and two teenaged sons. At the service, they were the only mourners, besides the still whimpering Letticia Franklin, who evidenced a genuine loss, one that the others, with their splendid minds, had difficulty imagining. His colleagues would attempt to dine out on anecdotes surrounding his departure, but Parkinson died quickly as a topic on the academic dinner party circuit. There simply wasn't enough to talk about—at least, not for publication. The classes he left behind were divided among faculty members too junior to complain, Erica among them. Soon, the most visible reminder of Parkinson's presence was the bloodstain on the carpet of the large and empty office no one wanted.

Chapter Eight

Doing what you wanted was the only training, and the only preliminary needed for doing more of what you wanted to do.
–Kingsley Amis, *Lucky Jim*

Erica sat at her desk, struggling through a sheaf of student papers. She groaned. Her officemate looked up from his work and asked, "That bad?"

"Pretty awful—and they weren't even mine 'til a month ago. As the resident maid of all work, I inherited one of Parkinson's classes."

"Not the Chaucer course?"

"No, thank goodness, John Crandall's got that. Lucky me, I've got an introduction to literature course. It seems that Parkinson spent most of the semester reading out loud to them."

"He *what?*"

"You heard me. The parents are paying a fortune in tuition for a college-level story hour. If they only knew."

"Are you carrying on in the Parkinsonian tradition?"

"I'm trying something a little more advanced. The students read the material *before* they get to class, and *then* we discuss it."

"A novel approach. How's it working out?"

"Some of the students had gotten very comfortable with the story-hour format, and they're not too happy about the new regime—but they're adapting, or they're failing." Erica reached for another stack of papers on her desk. "Speaking of the dreaded Chaucer course, it might interest you to know that Parkinson had the graduate students reading his entire critical output on the subject."

"Did he read it out loud to them?"

"No, this was a graduate course. They read it to themselves—no lips moving, I hope. Lucky for them, the old syllabus was scrapped when he—"

"Yes—"

"For which the students are eternally grateful."

Jamie gave Erica a sharp look.

"Not the dying part, Jamie. The part where they got a new course out of it."

"I see."

"Robin left her copy of the Parkinson opus here. Have you read any of his stuff?"

"A pleasure yet to come."

"A pleasure it is not. Even for academic prose, this is pretty turgid," Erica said. "A very tough read."

"It probably wouldn't appeal to you in any case," said Jamie, going back to his work. "Not your field, not your century."

"True, but even us twentieth-century types know abject pedantry when we see it. His stuff is painstaking, with the emphasis on the pain. Which, from what I understand, is the point of his last essay."

"The new sadism?"

"So you have been listening."

"I try to keep up," said Jamie.

"I haven't read it yet, but people are pretty excited about it. Whips and chains and *The Wife of Bath*. Pretty hot stuff." Erica paused for a moment, before continuing. "He must have had a major brainstorm before he died, because the rest of his output does not hold one in spellbinding awe."

"We all have to start somewhere."

"Jamie, this wasn't a start. This was most of his career."

"Well timed, wasn't it?" Jamie looked at Erica, a little longer than the question warranted. Abruptly, he asked, "I've been meaning to ask you to dinner."

Surprised by the invitation, Erica could only say, "And he cooks too? What a guy."

"If that would interest you."

"Sure," said Erica. "Some of my best friends are cooks."

"Next Friday, then? Eightish?"

"Okay. Yes. Thank you."

"Good. Do you know where I live?"

"I do. What can I bring?"

"Only yourself."

"I can manage that."

The conversation ended as both returned to their work. Shortly thereafter, Erica left to teach a class. A few minutes later, Jamie did the same, but not before he walked to her desk, picked up the pages that Robin had left behind, and dropped them into the bottom left-hand drawer of his desk. Given the usual state of Erica's desk, it would be weeks before she noticed they were missing, and months before she found them again.

Chapter Nine

AMANDA: I think very few people are completely normal really, deep down in their private lives. It all depends on a combination of circumstances. If all the
various cosmic thingummys fuse at the same moment,
and the right spark is struck, there's no telling what
one mightn't do.
–Noel Coward, *Private Lives*

Erica and Jamie had talked of many things, skillfully
avoiding the other's domestic arrangements. Erica was
fairly certain that someone or something kept Jamie's
home fires burning, but he, she, or it had not been pre-
sented for inspection. She knew that Jamie lived across
the river from Brixton, in a zip code where one talked
with the radicals and ate with the Tories. Erica, on the
Brixton side of the river, lived among the cultural elite
of more modest means and pretensions.

At the prescribed hour, bottle of wine in hand, Erica
pressed the buzzer next to the name "Bordwell," in-

scribed in calligraphy. If the lobby, understated in shades of mauve and gray, indicated things to come, then she would spend the rest of the evening being suitably impressed.

"Nice place. Do you own or rent?" Erica asked when Jamie opened his door to her.

"I'm in the process of buying, actually," said Jamie.

"So much for small talk," said Erica. "Let's eat."

"Not just yet. Why don't we open the wine and go from there?"

"It's white, it's chilled, it doesn't need to breathe."

"Yes, but I do," said Jamie.

On the way to the kitchen, Erica took a quick look around, surveying the living room that flowed gracefully into a dining area.

"Really nice digs, Jamie. You've done it in Art Noveau, haven't you?" asked Erica, noting the stylized curves and the Japanese influence on the furniture and attendant objects.

"How nice of you to notice," said Jamie.

"I adore anything Japanese," she said, "but Art Noveau is elitist, decadent—in the truest sense of the word—and espouses no higher ideal than 'I can afford this.' Didn't I see this place in last month's *House Beautiful?*"

"Did you see last month's *House Beautiful?*" he asked.

"Not last month's, no," said Erica.

In the kitchen, Jamie decanted the wine, while Erica continued her investigation. A picture framed in silver caught her attention, and she crossed the living room to examine it.

"Isn't this Brianna Bordwell? She's the news anchor on KNBC in L.A.? Your sister?"

"She was my wife," Jamie called from the kitchen.

"You were married to Brianna Bordwell?"

"She was married to me."

"I see."

"I'm surprised you recognized her."

"Jamie, I had a life before Brixton. I even worked for a living. Sometimes, that work took me to faraway places, like the West Coast."

"Of course, and you must tell me all about it." As he spoke, Jamie sautéed some vegetables. "For the last few years, Brianna and I have been bi-coastal, which is never easy."

"No," said Erica, swallowing her surprise. From what she had seen, discretion was the better part of everything for Jamie.

"Her picture is still in plain sight. Have you been divorced long?"

"Long enough."

"Amicably, I hope."

"How else would civilized adults end a marriage?"

"Based on the available evidence, I'd say somewhere between multiple stab wounds and a jaunty wave good-bye."

"That would seem to cover it. Some wine?"

Erica briefly wondered how advanced Jamie's thoughts were on the subject of alimony, particularly in cases where the wife had to be making more money than her spouse. She let that go.

Sipping her wine, Erica leaned against the doorjamb and watched Jamie cook. He looked very much at home standing over a hot stove, which she chose not to comment on, feeling equally at home in her position as an onlooker just outside the kitchen. Easing their way back into conversation, they turned to something sure-fire. In their profession, conversations could begin or end with the question "How is your teaching going?" Erica asked and Jamie answered.

"Well, I have been blessed with two teaching assistants in the Shakespeare survey, and an unlikelier pair is not to be imagined. One believes in a topical approach to Shakespeare, always in search of the lowest common denominator. From what I gather, she explained to her class that Richard III's problems stemmed from his inability to get a date."

"That's something our students would understand," said Erica.

"The other benighted soul is the most pious of creatures, who would vault the level of discourse into the heavens, if she could. She seems to have confused Shakespeare and God—"

"She's not alone in that. James Joyce did the same thing, adding himself to the equation."

"No doubt," said Jamie. "This one feels that, unworthy as she is (her words, not mine), she hopes to impart to the undergraduate population a true appreciation of what 'He' had in mind. She raises her eyes heavenward as she says it. The students are a little confused, and I'm left to untangle these wildly different 'approaches' before the final exam."

"You haven't tried to straighten out these two?"

"Our time together is limited, alas. Both of them are going on next semester to teach a freshman writing course—unsupervised, I might add."

"That's a scary thought," said Erica.

"Given the state of things, what's wrong with what

either one of them is trying to do?" asked Jamie. "Neither runs the risk of being politically incorrect. They don't make enough sense to offend, and they have lots of enthusiasm—possibly zeal, in one case. It might just get them a job someday." Jamie lowered the heat on the burner. "For the time being, the study guides may be a bit odd, but they're neatly typed and on time. I have no real complaints."

"Such rigorous standards," said Erica. "How do you maintain them?"

Jamie was too engaged in his cooking to answer.

For a moment, Erica considered in seriousness what he offered, she hoped, in jest. The politically correct were out in force, monitoring freedom of thought in ways that made McCarthyism look meek by comparison. Perhaps the meek had inherited the earth after all. Conscientious objectors were silenced. If they failed to practice what they were supposed to preach, they faced a bleak future of unpublished articles leading to the dead end of no promotion, no tenure, no job. Erica could plead ignorance, but she knew as well as anyone the way things were. What she would do with this knowledge remained to be seen. She knew what Jamie was doing: publishing whatever he could, as fast as his flying fingers could type. He would never lack advancement.

"How's your man?" Erica asked.

"Who?"

"You know, the poet of choice. The one who never leaves the library."

"He's still there. Still deep in conversation with famous men, transcribing his chats in a series of leatherbound diaries. I'm reading through the accumulated

writings in an attempt to sort the factual from the fic-
tive. He's much more interesting in conversation with
people he never met."

"What a way to live."

"His or mine?"

"Both?"

At a point, they moved from the kitchen to the dining
room, making the progression from the professional to
the personal, from report to rapport.

"Do you have any family?" Jamie asked.

"Actually, I emerged full blown from my father's
forehead," Erica answered.

"Just like the goddess Athena. How nice for you. Is
there a significant other—"

"Boyfriend, beau, spousal unit, great and good
friend—"

"Yes, and so on. I imagine you with someone named
Nick."

"Nick?" asked Erica, as she helped herself to more
chicken. "As in, drinks beer and squashes the can on
his head?"

"No, I was thinking more along the lines of a Nick
Charles."

"The detective? Witty, urbane, alcoholic? My type
exactly."

"I meant no offense."

"None taken. In any case, that would make me Nora.
Not Ibsen's Nora—Hammett's Nora, Lillian Hellman,
Myrna Loy. I can live with that, but I don't."

"Speaking of which, you live with . . ." Jamie waited
for Erica to fill in the blank.

"I live with myself," she said. "We argue."

"Who's we?"

"We? We is me. I live alone, and have ever since I came back to Brixton."

"Yes, that's right. You were a graduate student here. I'm surprised we never met."

"I did my degree on the installment plan, sort of a correspondence course. When I decided that it was time to finish, I hid in the library and cranked out the dissertation. Then the teaching job came up, and I'm still here. That's the short version," she added.

"What about the one you left behind? The Friday afternoon departures? To New York, wasn't it?"

"You sly devil. You don't miss a thing, do you?"

"Not as a rule."

"Well, neither did I. I didn't miss a single one of those meetings. I would have thought that people had better things to do on a Friday afternoon."

"You don't enjoy the company of the senior faculty?"

"I didn't say that, but I could do without a few of their quirks. We could begin with Sander Small."

"The Sandman?"

"At every meeting, he would make the same speech. Short or long, depending on the number of items on the agenda. Always the same speech about how junior faculty should never use the first person in their scholarly writing. As far as he was concerned, the "I's" definitely didn't have it. Then he would rest. Literally. I spent too many Friday afternoons watching him nod off, slowly, slowly, his head sinking into his chest until he almost fell asleep, then saving himself at the last moment, pulling his head upright in a single, swanlike motion."

"I'll miss the Sandman," said Jamie. "I hope his retirement is wearing well."

"I'm sure it's restful," said Erica. "Anyway, I was always there when I needed to be."

"No criticism intended—and no trips this year, it seems."

"No, sadly. This year, the trip would be pointless, unless I want to visit an empty apartment. The visitee is away."

"How far?"

"Very far. London."

"He's a diplomat?"

"Guess again."

"Doctor, lawyer, Indian chief?"

"An actor," said Erica.

"I thought you had better sense. How did that happen?" Jamie asked.

"We met on a commercial shoot."

Jamie looked blank.

"You know, shooting a commercial—like shooting an elephant, only different."

Jamie winced and poured more wine.

"In a previous life, as you know, I wrote ad copy, and for a while I specialized in household products. One particular commercial featured a dad and daughter bonding over floor wax, a mop, and a bucket. You know—Mom's out, so let's surprise her with a clean, shiny floor. What Dad was doing at home during the day was not really an issue at the time, more of an economic indicator."

"It could have been a Saturday," said Jamie.

"It wasn't," said Erica. "Anyway, dad and daughter reach for the mop and bucket, and in a matter of seconds, the floor is glowing, as if it had been sealed in something radioactive, which it may have been. Mom walks in, carrying her briefcase, the signature touch so we know she was at work, and everybody's happy—quality time with the kid and a clean floor into the bargain. Alan played the dad, in case you hadn't guessed."

"Alan?"

"Alan DeLorme."

"Alan DeLorme," Jamie repeated, "never heard of him," he said dismissively.

"I don't think he's ever heard of you, either," Erica said, then quickly continued, "He's in London with a production of *Othello*. You may have read about it. It began in Central Park, then moved to Broadway, and now London. It's unusual that they're letting members of the New York cast perform in London. They, being the British equivalent of Equity, the actor's union. Acting jobs are scarce, and they don't usually give them to foreign competition—at least, not without a fight. In the case of people with big-name status, which obviously doesn't apply to Alan, and for those who are deemed irreplaceable—which it seems he is—then the actor's union will make an exception."

"What part does he play?" asked Jamie, with the look of a man whose political correctness might be on the line.

"Oh, didn't I say? He was born to play Iago."

"You date the personification of motiveless malignity?"

"It's called acting, Jamie."

"As long as it's not typecasting."

"It isn't, but thanks for asking. The chicken was delicious, by the way."

"Thank you, Erica. You're not a cook, I take it?"

"No, I buy food on more of a need-to-eat basis. When I see the word *clarify,* I think they're talking about writing—but I'm very good at cleaning up," she said, indicating toward the kitchen.

"That won't be necessary. Shall we move into the other room?"

"How many rooms do you have?"

"A few."

"What a stunning view of the river," she said as they made their way into the living room, balancing glasses and dessert plates. Jamie picked up the conversation.

"How long has he been away?"

Still on that, are we? Erica thought, as she spooned in a healthy dose of crème brule.

"A while," she replied.

"How much longer will he be staying?"

"A while longer."

"What's he like?"

"Like? I don't know. I'm not asked to describe him that often. He's a wonderful actor, but he'll probably never play Hamlet. He's got what I like to think of as craggy good looks, but he's not a pretty boy. He's more of a character actor, so aging isn't really an issue for him."

"Do you miss him?"

"Not much. I call his answering machine now and again to hear the sound of his voice."

"Do you leave messages?"

"No, and the machine is voice-activated, so it doesn't register the click of a hang up."

"There would be a lot of clicks, I take it?"

"Enough. Actually, the worst part of a long-distance relationship is the way you tend to mythologize the departed—"

"That's a nice way of putting it," said Jamie. "You could also get bored and move on—"

"I could, but for the time being I'm managing in my splendid isolation, with plenty of time for reflection and contemplation."

"What are you contemplating?" Jamie asked.

"I'm not sure what you mean," Erica answered.

"No one local strikes your fancy?"

"No," she said, surprised at the question. "I haven't lived here that long, and I don't know too many people outside the Department. Most of the people I knew in graduate school saw the light early and got on the first bus to law school—but you were asking me about the available talent."

"Was I?"

"Well, it is not exactly thick upon the ground—present company excluded, of course. The Department seems to specialize in men who are unavailable, uninteresting, or just plain dead."

"No more than any other academic department."

"One mysterious death per year is the average?"

"Erica, what are you talking about?"

"Parkinson, of course. Was there another?"

"Was there one?" asked Jamie. "Erica, people die. It's natural order of things. Granted, Parkinson died in a way that was unnatural for most people, but quite right for him, if you think about it."

"I do think about it."

"Erica, we were all shocked by the sudden passing of Professor Parkinson—but to my knowledge, there was no mystery."

"Thank you for the boilerplate condolences, Jamie. I already heard them at Parkinson's memorial. The thing I find mysterious," she continued, "is why no one finds any of this odd. Parkinson left the Department feet first, after they separated him from his dictionary, and it's strictly business as usual. Reassign his courses, sweep everything under the rug, pretend it never happened."

"What I find mysterious," said Jamie, "is why any of this matters to you. Did you know him well?"

"No, almost not at all. Now, though, it seems that if you wanted to kill him, you had to take a number. At the memorial service it occurred to me that not a few of the people in attendance were there just to make sure that he was very dead. So I wondered if anyone had helped to make him that way."

"Erica, really—such talk! It was a nasty death, but his fault entirely."

"His fault? Not an accident? Are we blaming the victim?"

"Listen to me, Erica. I expect that deaths by dictionary are pretty rare, so the insurance company has a new statistic for its tables. As far as I know, the police have not been heard from since the fateful day, so I assume they are satisfied. None of this should concern you."

"Maybe not. At the memorial service, Mark Gorman and Larry O'Brien seemed awfully chummy. They even glared in unison. Are they an item?"

"Not to my knowledge—and not, I think, to the knowledge of Larry's wife and three children," said Jamie.

"So why are they buddies all of a sudden?" asked Erica.

"Mark decided to take on Larry's tenure case as a cause célèbre."

"So he feels he must right a terrible wrong?"

"No, he's found a new way to exasperate the Department and perhaps even annoy the Administration."

"Sounds perfect."

"That's how he fills *his* time," Jamie said. "We were discussing more productive ways of filling yours. It's early in your career, and you're young—"

"I have seen thirty," said Erica.

"And a lovely sight it is. But bear in mind, it's never too early to publish. You could begin by turning your dissertation into a book. Forgive me, I forgot the topic. It's about?"

"It's about two-hundred pages. Oh, the title? 'Female Playwrights of the Twentieth Century Who Are Still Breathing.' I paraphrase."

Jamie ignored the sarcasm. "If professional advancement doesn't appeal to you, there's always your personal life."

"Oh?"

"If you want to develop a borderline obsession with an unsuspecting male, you might try one who, like your female playwrights, is still breathing."

"Excuse me?"

"Perhaps you would care to join me in the other room?"

Erica paused for a moment before responding. "You not suggesting we retire to the library for brandy and cigars, are you?"

"I'm suggesting that we retire, but not to the library."

"Is this a joke?"

"Hardly."

"Do you say this to all the girls?"

"What do you think?"

"I think we don't know ourselves well enough."

"Know ourselves?" His laugh sounded like a cough

exploding in his throat. "Luckily, that's not a require-ment. We don't even have to know each other, though I think we do. Only too well. More wine?"

"I think I've had enough."

"Suit yourself," he said, pouring himself another glass.

"Jamie, it may have escaped your attention, but peo-ple don't jump in and out of bed with reckless abandon anymore."

"Erica, you needn't worry. Neither of us is infected with anything other than vaulting ambition."

"That may be true," she agreed, "but actions do have the most unfortunate habit of coming with conse-quences."

"So do inactions."

"So I'm damned if I do, damned if I don't?" Erica asked.

"No," Jamie answered. "I was simply suggesting a pleasurable end to a pleasant evening. Take your mind off—whatever—strictly recreational."

"You mean, for the exercise? Have you considered taking up squash?"

"I happen to be the club champion."

Of course, said Erica to herself.

"I have considered many possibilities," said Jamie.

I haven't considered enough, thought Erica, who had somehow forgotten that the pattern of fine dining often leads from soup to seduction.

"So it's eat, drink, and be merry," said Erica, "and now we're up to the merry part."

"Like Lewis Carroll's definition of a word, it means whatever you want it to mean," said Jamie.

I am in the presence of a past master of sangfroid, thought Erica, for the moment more impressed than angry. "An offer this offhand could hardly be construed as harassment," she began.

"Which it most certainly isn't," he finished.

"Of course not. Never." She paused. "You know, I thought this was the beginning of a beautiful friendship, but it seems to be the end."

"Not at all," said Jamie. "You needn't worry. It won't come up again."

Erica was tempted to say something more, but decided it was time to go. "Well, I should be off, before it gets too late." Grabbing her purse, she said, "Thank you, Jamie, for . . . the evening." Under the circumstances, a reciprocal invitation seemed out of the question.

"My pleasure," he said as he escorted her, with some haste, to the elevator.

Over my dead body, she thought, as the door closed between them.

Chapter Ten

Western wind, when wilt thou blow,
The small rain down can rain?
Christ, if my love were in my arms
And I in my bed again!
–Anonymous, "Western Wind"

Erica had not misread a situation this completely since her first encounter with modern poetry. In the long term, she would distance herself from the man who sat at the desk across from her. In the short term, there was only one thing to do: she went to the gym.

Fueled by the desire to get rid of a distinctly non-sexual frustration, Erica found her way to the House of Pain early the next morning. The House of Pain was not a place but a class, ninety minutes of competitive agony. Strangely enough, most of the participants were women. The first sixty minutes emphasized strength, which the male participants could manage, grunting and sweating with the girls. The last half hour required flexibility, an area in which men can sometimes find themselves challenged. Never having been taught, they had to learn it for themselves or find another class.

Erica was brave enough to face the House of Pain, but not the showers. The gym was run on an economy plan with cleaning seen as a frill—or worse, a sign of weakness. Instead, she dressed quickly and left, preferring the facilities at home. According to custom, as soon as the apartment door was closed, she began to disrobe, dropping her clothes, like Hansel and Gretel's breadcrumbs, in a line behind her. The clothes usually found their way to the hamper, though occasionally, depending on how the day had gone, she considered dropping them in the nearest incinerator.

Moving with deliberate speed through her apartment, Erica halted at the bathroom door. Inside, the water was running and the shower in use, its occupant betrayed by an affection for Gilbert and Sullivan and a misplaced confidence in his singing ability. Underdressed for a confrontation, Erica retreated to the bedroom where she found, on the floor, an overnight bag tagged by British Airlines, its contents decorating her bed. Heart pounding, she returned to the bathroom, entered quickly, and slammed the door.

"Eeeek!" she screamed with horror-film intensity. "There's a man in my shower!"

"Erica, you scared me to death," Alan said, clutching the shower curtain for dear life.

"I scared you? How do you think I feel?"

"Surprised?"

"And then some. What are you doing here?"

"Why don't you join me, and I'll tell you all about it."

"I thought you'd never ask."

Chapter Eleven

Think you there was, or might be, such a man
As this I dreamed of?
–William Shakespeare, *Anthony and Cleopatra*

Explanations were not immediately forthcoming.

"It's been too long," Erica said.

"Try and restrain your enthusiasm," Alan said. "Guess I'm just lucky to find you at home. Where were you this morning?"

"I went to the gym to get the kinks out."

"Not all of them, I hope."

"Never. You didn't lose your keys, I see."

"I'm sorry I startled you."

"Alan, dear, I was considering a variation on the shower scene from *Psycho*."

"With me as Janet Leigh. A comforting thought, especially after I've come all this way."

"Yes, you have, haven't you?" said Erica. "To what

do I owe the honor? The water drowned you out in the shower, and after a while, I stopped listening."

"So I noticed."

"Ticket sales take a nose dive?"

"Actually, sales continue to be brisk," said Alan. "I have been summoned. Flown in, first class."

"Really? Who wants to see you?"

"Would you care to rephrase that question?"

"Who—with that kind of money—requested your presence in this time zone? It is this time zone, isn't it? You're not selling out to Hollywood, are you?"

"So fast it would make your head spin."

"Not," she said, again in mock horror, "*television*."

"We talkin' features, babe."

"So who died and made you a hot commodity?"

"Erica, honey, thank you for your support."

"Hey, I knew you when."

"When was that?"

"When you were underemployed, Mop Man."

"Thank you very much."

"Come on, now. Don't play hurt. Just tell me everything, and don't skip any details."

"Well," said Alan, easing himself into a more comfortable position. "The director is the latest wunderkind. His name doesn't mean much outside of Sundance, where he won enough prizes for a major studio to hand him a ton of money and a script. He caught *Othello* in the Park and wants to talk to me about a part."

"What kind of part?"

"Like Iago, I'm guessing, if that's what he saw me do—something reptilean, probably."

"This isn't a heavy make-up job, is it? We are speaking in the metaphorical sense," asked Erica.

"Is there any other?" Alan replied.

"Don't forget, the snake has all the best lines."

"I just hope that the snake doesn't get tired of saying them."

"A little early to be worrying about typecasting, isn't it? You have to be a type first."

"I thought I was your type," he said.

"True, very true," she answered. "So when do you see the boy wonder? Are his parents letting him stay up extra late to talk to you?"

"Not on a school night, no. We meet on Monday in New York. Did I mention he plans to film in New York? I think there's a clause in his contract about egg cremes."

"Will there be a problem getting out of your *Othello* contract?"

"Getting a little ahead of ourselves, aren't we?"

"It would be great, though."

"Yes, Erica, it would."

"And you came all this way to see me."

"Yes," said Alan, "they paid my way to New York. After that, I'm on my own."

"This is turning out to be a pretty nifty weekend after all," Erica said. "Two hot dates in two days. Most weekends, I make Emily Dickinson look like a social animal."

"Another hot date?" he asked.

"To tell you the truth, I didn't realize it was a hot date until it was too late. I had dinner with a colleague."

"What was on the menu?"

"Some chicken thing, with spices," Erica said, "and vegetables, sauteed or something. I brought the wine."

"Have you considered a career in a restaurant reviewing?"

"The food was good. What more do you want?"

"And for dessert?"

"Me, actually. Well, me and the crème brulee, though not necessarily in that order."

"Oh, really."

"Yes," she said, drawing out the word.

"Do I have reason to be jealous? What's he like, this guy?"

"Tall, blond, handsome—your basic nightmare," said Erica. She then reiterated the terms of Jamie's modest proposal.

"And what did you do?" he asked as Erica reached the climax of her story.

"I cut him off at the pass."

"I suppose that's preferable to being cut off at the knees."

"That was Plan B."

"You have to admit, he has style," said Alan. " 'Dessert? Coffee? Bed? No? Good-bye.' Kind of minimalist, but as a technique, I'll have to keep it in mind."

"Yes, you never know when it might come in handy. How is the fair Desdemona?"

"God's gift to the theater? Believe me, I barely register on her consciousness. Last I heard, she was dating a minor member of the Royal Family."

"You can act her off the stage."

"Well, modesty forbids . . ." he said, trailing off. "As far as she's concerned, the rest of the cast are strictly walking scenery. I'd strangle her myself, but Othello always beats me to it."

"And what is strangulation but a reverse form of embrace?"

"Not in this case."

"The show must go on."

"And it does," said Alan. "In fact, my understudy, Eve Harrington, has been off his head with joy ever since he learned that I'd be missing the weekend performances. Playing Ludovico doesn't fulfill his true potential."

"Ludovico?"

"An attendant lord, one that will do to swell a progress. This Brit is hoping against hope that I'll be gunned down by one of the crazed lunatics roaming the sidewalks of American cities. Just like in the movies."

Relieved to hear about the state of Anglo-American affairs, Erica said, "Poor little Eve. He's going to be crushed when you survive this trip."

"Hey, it's a tough business. He's got to get used to disappointments," Alan replied. "I'm really more interested in the events of last evening. What do you think brought this on? The Jamesian tension get to be too much for you?"

"Would that be Frank or Jesse?"

"Henry, actually. You're not the only one who ever read a book, you know."

"The Jamesian tension," she repeated. "Hmm, let me think. At the time, I think we were talking about the dead guy in the Department—always a turn on."

Alan looked confused.

"You know, the one who—the dictionary. I wrote you about him."

"Oh, *that* dead guy."

"Speaking of writing, honey—not that I don't love the letters with the nifty stamps—but there's this thing called email that I think you're really going to like."

"So you say. I want to get back to your little talk with the friendly colleague. I have only one question. What were you thinking?"

"Haven't we gotten to the point where a man and a woman who work together can have dinner in a non-public place without the assumption that one or the other should have known better?" asked Erica.

"Let me rephrase the question," said Alan. "What were you thinking?"

"To tell you the truth, I don't know what his sudden and totally unexpected offer was about, irresistible as I am."

"So what prompted this charming proposition?"

"At the time, I was questioning the conventional wisdom that a dictionary lands on someone's head without help."

"You mean, did it jump or was it pushed?"

"Something like that."

"Maybe the deceased was practicing a stunt for the next faculty party," said Alan.

"This guy wasn't much of a party person," Erica replied, "though I did see him at a social event just before he died."

"What did your little friend have to say?"

"He thinks it comes under the category of my filling the time available with morbid thoughts."

"There may be some truth in that."

"Possibly. I just can't help feeling that something odd is going on. I mean, the dead guy was a jerk, and that's about the nicest thing anyone has said about him—at least, among the things that are true. Then he died, and people just couldn't forget him fast enough. These are people who, at best, can agree to disagree. There seems to be some sort of unspoken contract, and the bottom line is that none of this ever happened."

"What's so strange about that?" Alan asked. "It's kind of awkward and maybe a little embarrassing when one of your own goes out balancing a dictionary between his eyebrows."

"It's more than bad form on his part. I'm not explaining this very well."

"Not yet, no."

"It's like the curious incident of the dog that didn't bark," said Erica.

"I know this one. It's Sherlock Holmes, *The Hound of the Baskervilles*."

"No, my dear Watson. Everyone gets that wrong. It's Sherlock Holmes, but the dog that was notable for its lack of commotion is from *The Silver Blaze*."

"I'm willing to take your word for it."

"Very kind of you."

"Still, you're concerned because people aren't barking?" Alan smiled, a little nervously. "We're not talking about the m-word are we?"

"Which m-word did you have in mind?"

"You think somebody murdered this guy?"

"I try not to. I just wonder if it was as accidental an accident as everybody seems to think."

"Erica, passion and planning make it murder. From

what you've told me, these people don't get too worked up about much of anything, unless it's the heterosexist tradition in high Icelandic love songs."

"That's pretty good, Alan."

"Thank you," he said, looking pleased by her compliment. "Do you really think that this guy had something, or did something, that someone else would kill for?"

"You're right," she said. "It's not like we're dealing with actors."

"Heavens, no."

"The dead guy's main claim to fame, other than his deadness, is an article he wrote, his last one, on *The Wife of Bath's Tale.*"

"The what?" asked Alan.

"That's Chaucer, for the uninitiated."

"So initiate me," he said.

"I'll spare you the particulars. Let's just say that the dead guy's getting kind of famous as a result—as famous as a medievalist gets," said Erica.

"I see." Alan paused. "And have the police been heard from?"

"They put in an appearance."

"The school isn't worked up about this?"

"Not so you'd notice."

"The family isn't screaming for vengeance?"

"Not as yet."

"And he's still dead?"

"Very."

"Let me see if I've got this straight," Alan began. "In your spare time, you wonder about a murderer that has escaped the notice of everyone but you."

"I'm pretty sure it got the dead guy's attention."

"Well, he's not talking, and neither is anyone else."

"Nope."

"You're nearing the end of your contract, right? And you initiate conversations about dead guys?"

"It's preferable to initiating conversations with dead guys, but if you put it that way—"

"How far has the stain of corruption spread?" Alan asked.

"The what?"

"Well, Erica, does the murderer live in your midst, or was it an outsider? Did they call in a specialist?"

"Very funny, Alan."

"You're a pretty tight little group," he continued. "Have you found any likely suspects? Any disgruntled medievalists on the payroll?"

"At the moment, there's only one medievalist in the Department, and he would not be voted most likely to wield a murder weapon. John Crandall—kind of a scrawny little guy, close-cropped hair, prisoner-of-war pallor. He doesn't look like he could lift the *OED,* much less commit mayhem with it."

"O.E.D.?"

"The *Oxford English Dictionary* as blunt instrument."

"I see," said Alan. "Erica, you know I trust your intuition, but this scenario has a few holes in it."

"Is this your tactful way of talking me out of this?"

"I have never tired to talk you out of anything."

"Alan, if you plan to tell me that this is nothing to worry my pretty little head about, someone beat you to it."

"Then he must not know you very well. I value my life far too much ever to make that suggestion. Just be careful, okay? These people—your 'colleagues' as you put it—I don't know what they'd kill for. I don't want to know. Do you?"

"Probably not. Let's drop it. I guess I just needed a reality check."

"I'm just the guy to give it to you."

"Sounds good," she said, "I'm glad to see that the jet lag hasn't gotten to you. How long are you staying, by the way?"

"I have no plans for the next twenty-four hours," he said. "I'm not keeping you from anything, am I?"

"I have no plans to leave this particular spot."

"That presents certain opportunities. What about food?"

"I'm a little low on provisions," Erica began.

"Tell me something I don't know," Alan said, as he got out of bed and headed for the door.

"Where are you going?" she asked.

"To find the number of the nearest Chinese restaurant," he said.

"It's taped to the phone."

"With the rest of the emergency numbers?"

"All vital information," Erica said.

"I had forgotten your curious relationship with food. Too few people look upon an oatmeal cookie as health food."

"Hey, they sometimes have raisins in them, which are supposed to be good for you," said Erica. "I intend to enjoy the years or months or minutes I have left before my metabolism crashes and gravity has its way with me."

"Gravity can get in line."

"Before we take numbers, could you call the restaurant? Ask for the usual. They know me."

"Done and done," said Alan when he completed the call.

"The food won't be here for a bit," said Erica.

"However will we fill the time?" asked Alan.

"I have an idea," said Erica. "Come here." Alan resumed his position. "Now, relax, and don't think of England."

"What should I think of?" he wanted to know.

"Only me."

Chapter Twelve

My first thought was, he lied in every word . . .
—Robert Browning, "Childe Roland to the Dark
Tower Came"

Between food deliveries and making up for lost time, Alan's departure, the next afternoon, came sooner than expected. They talked as they waited for his cab to arrive.

"Are they making any noise about reappointing you?" Alan asked.

"Yes," Erica replied. "Barnyard sounds. Animal noises."

"When will you know for sure?"

"They're beginning to put some effort into finding a medievalist to replace the dead guy. They should get to me after that."

"Let me offer a thought, and let me finish before you get insulted."

"This sounds promising."

"Just listen. You know, I've never really understood why you're in this business in the first place."

"I'm in it for the vacations, of course. All that free time in which to starve."

"Not for the teaching? Or for the students? No interest in molding young minds?"

"I don't want to mold anybody's anything," she said with some firmness.

"Sorry."

"No, I'm sorry. It's just there are a few people—good teachers, some of them—who get their emotional jollies from a roomful of adoring children. Or think they're taking the high road because they wait until the little lads and ladies are juniors before they ask them out." She paused. "Not my favorite people."

"I can see that. Women too?"

"We've come a long way, baby. One senior colleague—female—greets the new women in the Department with tales of how she used to indulge in a few extra-extra-curricular activities during her early years at Brixton. She's safely married now, but if she were still up to her old tricks, I'm pretty sure she'd be up to them somewhere else."

"Who is she?"

"There's no point in naming names. You don't know her."

"Forget her name. I want her phone number."

"You're too old for her."

"Forget it," said Alan. "Now we know why she's here. Why are you here?"

"To add my light to the sum of light?"

"Not the answer I expected," said Alan. "Really?"

"In a way," Erica replied. "Once upon a time, intellectuals talked about sharing in the community of knowledge. Now, we've forgotten the kindergarten skill of sharing well with others. We prefer to keep it to ourselves, or sell to the highest bidder. If there are any."

"You lost me at the 'highest-bidder' part," said Alan. "So, let me jump in. You and I both know you could do something else, and for big bucks too," he added. "You just don't seem too thrilled with this place."

"Thank you, kind sir. You really think I'm inching over the edge, don't you?"

"No, no," said Alan, though his voice could have used a little more conviction. "You just seem a little alone here. Have you spoken to anyone in your family about this?"

"Alan, you know what my family is like. We used to be the kind who wrote once a year. Now we write once a year and don't mail the letters."

"I just think you might consider your options."

"That's nice and vague. What do you mean exactly?"

"I'm certainly not the best person to offer advice, career or otherwise, and you never needed anyone else to jumpstart you career."

"I wasn't aware it had stalled," said Erica, coolly.

"Maybe it hasn't," Alan said carefully. "That would be up to you to decide. It's just that Brixton might not be the place for you. If memory serves, the master plan, before you got the last-minute appointment, was to get the degree and skip town."

"I remember. My bags were packed. I was ready to go."

"Erica, I have always thought of you as a spunky, go-your-own-way kind of a gal, but I would have to think that conversations pushing in the direction of how the dead guy in the department got that way probably won't lead to career advancement. If you want to get fired, I'm all for it. If not, think about what you're doing. Maybe there is a huge conspiracy throbbing under the calm exterior of Brixton's English Department, and maybe not. Either way, you could find yourself in deeper than you want to be."

"How deep is that?"

"How about professionally compromised? Or personally at risk?"

Erica started to speak, but Alan stopped her.

"I don't mean daggers drawn, or whatever they do to settle a score."

"Daggers would be about right," said Erica. "Even if they're only looking daggers at someone—or pistols raised at twenty paces, that might work."

"My concern is not them, it's you. Just think about what kind of game you're playing here, and why."

"I'll keep it in mind."

"Good," he said, as the sound of a honking taxi interrupted them.

"Give my best to the Beave," she said.

"You know I will."

"I won't ask when you'll be back," said Erica.

"Good choice," Alan replied, " 'cause I don't know."

"Saying good-bye is harder than I thought it would be," Erica said, the strain showing. "If you don't mind, I won't accompany you to the curb. I don't want the neighbors to see the tracks of my tears."

"No problem," Alan said. "The sight of that robe would be enough to scandalize anyone."

"What do you mean?" she asked, looking down at her outfit.

"Do you think it's time to throw it out?" he asked.

"Flannel is forever," she answered, "and besides, it's black-watch plaid—"

"Just like your favorite dress in the fourth grade, I know—which, by the looks of it, is about as long as you've owned that thing." Again, they heard the honking.

"I've got to go."

Another honk, more insistent this time. "He'll wait," she said.

"Not forever," said Alan, kissing her quickly as he shouldered the overnight bag. "Well, think lovely thoughts, and watch out for falling dictionaries," he said as he walked out the door.

"It's an occupational hazard, but I'll do what I can," Erica said, more to herself than to his departing figure. "That much I'm sure of."

Chapter Thirteen

Illiterate him, I say, quite from your memory.
–Richard Brinsley Sheridan, *The Rivals*

On Monday morning, when Sarah asked about the weekend, Erica answered with her usual, "Same old, same old." Sarah sighed and looked at her friend.

"You cease to exist on weekends, don't you?" said Sarah.

Erica nodded, thinking it safer to agree, and with more than a sneaking suspicion that she should be offended by Sarah's remark. For two people whose paths crossed three times a week, they were reasonably forthcoming about their lives, but they were proceeding slowly towards full disclosure. The details of the weekend with Alan, like last week's laundry, remained unsorted. Her dinner with Jamie would require an explanation she did not have.

"A misery statistic in the making," said Erica, as they walked in the direction of the mailroom. Turning the corner, they came upon Professors Leventhal and Grayson-Grossman in a whispering confab presided over by Elaine.

"Is this a secret meeting or can anyone join in?" asked Erica. Two of the three acknowledged Sarah and Erica with nods and a minimum of dialogue, departing together. Sarah checked her mailbox and also made a hasty exit. Elaine stayed behind to chat.

"Do I know how to clear a room, or do I know how to clear a room?" Erica asked.

"You do," Elaine answered, "though it was the tail end of our discussion."

"I'm beginning to think that those two communicate in a language twins teach each other," Erica said.

"The Geminis. Very possibly," said Elaine. "They still use English for public occasions. We were regaling each other with horror stories from hiring committees past."

"How is that going?" asked Erica, with more than a little interest.

"There's one young woman in particular who looks promising for the medievalist position," Elaine said. "We'll interview her, along with about a dozen others, at the MLA convention in December. What am I saying? A few weeks from now."

"Tell me, Elaine, is the Brixton English Department finally ready to cross the color line?"

"Erica, you know we would if we could. We'd be thrilled if a black Ph.D. looked our way, or any qualified person of color, but so far there have been no takers."

"Elaine, at Brixton, 'person of color' means the rich kids after Winter Break. That goes for the faculty too."

"We're doing what we can," Elaine insisted. "It just

takes time and care. Our timing just hasn't worked out, and maybe we need to be a little more careful."

"Really?"

"Our friends told me an interesting anecdote. It seems that during the process of her hiring, the late Professor Parkinson sidled up to candidate Grayson-Grossman (I think she was just Grayson then, or was it Grossman?) and when he had her alone . . ."

"Yes?" said Erica, fascinated.

"Well, according to her, and I quote, he whispered 'unspeakable things' to her."

"What did he say exactly?"

"She did not specify—we were interrupted," she added, smiling at Erica. "I'd never heard this before, but Stew obviously had."

"She took the job," said Erica. "She must have gotten over it."

"Yes, but Stew hasn't. He kept repeating that she didn't have to worry about him—about Parkinson—anymore."

"That Parkinson really was the life of the party, wasn't he?"

"You have no idea," said Elaine. "I'll tell you about it another time. I must go teach now," she said, checking her watch.

"You have to wonder what Parkinson could have said to make an eighteenth-century scholar blush," said Erica, walking with Elaine out of the mailroom. "They did not spare the innuendo in that century."

"If I'm not mistaken, Professor Grayson-Grossman specializes in the works of Alexander Pope. 'Moderation in all things.'"

"She would," said Erica.

Chapter Fourteen

Why did you bring these daggers from the place?
  –William Shakespeare, *Macbeth*

Erica retreated to her office to organize her thoughts before the day's teaching. She had shifted her office hours to avoid an overlap with Jamie's. Few of her students had noticed the change, so she saw less of them. Their visits, as a rule, were generally limited to those critical moments before or after a paper was due. One student had noticed the time change, however, and arranged his schedule to fit hers.

"Ned," said Erica to the figure standing in her doorway, a little surprised to see him there alone.

"Do you have a minute?"

"Of course," she said. "Come in."

"Do you mind if I close the door?"

Erica's heart sank. This request coming from a student usually preceded the type of revelation best left unspoken, especially on a Monday morning.

"Sure, go ahead," said Erica, trying to sound nonchalant. He closed the door and entered the room, but remained standing.

"What can I do for you?" she asked. "Please, have a seat."

He continued to stand, saying, "There's something I want to show you." He put down his backpack and began to unbutton his shirt.

"Ned?"

"Oh, sorry," he said, turning his back to her.

Too stunned to say anything, Erica watched from the back as he quickly worked his way down the row of buttons, loosened his belt, lowered his zipper, and carefully pulled something from his pants.

"*Ned?*" she said again, this time with emphasis.

"Just a second, I've almost got it," he said. In a flash, he whirled around to face her, quickly readjusting his clothes as he placed on her desk a thin paperback book. She looked from the white rectangle, to him, and back again.

"What is this?"

"I know it looks pretty weird," said Ned, sitting down. "Let me explain before you call security."

"I don't plan to call anyone," said Erica, knowing it would be days before security found them. "What exactly is going on?"

"You remember that Robin and I are in the Chaucer class."

"Yes," said Erica, as more of a question than an answer.

"Right," said Ned, as if settling the matter for himself. "Well, Crandall took it over after Parkinson died. He's pretty good in class. He really knows his stuff."

"That's nice to hear about John. Could we get to the point?"

"Sure, sorry," said Ned. "He assigned a term paper that's due before the break. No late papers. He's a real stickler about that sort of thing."

"Ned, the point?"

"Right. I've been hearing the buzz about the last essay Parkinson did, and I thought I'd check it out. See if I could be inspired. I guess you think I'm turning into the typical graduate student."

"Not typical, not at all," said Erica.

"I haven't become a regular grind, not yet anyway. I was just curious, and desperate for ideas. I don't have a lot of thoughts about *The Canterbury Tales.*"

"Most people don't. Could we cut to the chase?"

"Sure, okay. I went to the library and called up Parkinson's article on the computer catalogue, which sent me to the reference room in the basement of the library. You know where they keep the periodicals. I found the most recent edition of *Chauceriana,* untouched by human hands, judging from the dust. What a literary detective. I thought I was the first one in my class to grab this hot piece of news, until I opened the journal. I didn't have to look up the article in the table of contents. I could see where it *was*—emphasis on the past tense. See for yourself."

Ned opened the book for her. Someone had cut a neat line along the glued binding and taken out about twenty pages at the center of the journal. All of Parkinson's work had been excised except for the last page of notes, which in his case were always copious. As Erica fingered it, the page fell onto the pile of papers on her desk.

It was the longest unbroken speech that Ned had ever made in her presence. Now Erica was lost for words.

"I know, periodicals are not supposed to leave the reference room," he said. "They check backpacks on the way out of the library. I had to hide it under my shirt. My belt kept it from slipping."

"You wore it out?"

"It was the only way. I thought you should see it."

"Why?"

"I didn't want to make a federal case out of it. I mean, people rip off the library all the time. This is different."

This is different, thought Erica, but she did not want to infect Ned with her curiosity. Trying to downplay the situation, she said, "It's not like this is the only copy in captivity. Any of the schools in the area would get this journal, not to mention a few subscribers."

"It was the only copy in our library," he said.

"Maybe someone else in your class got the same idea you did," she said, "and he or she wanted the article for home use."

"It just seemed weird to me," Ned insisted.

Erica decided this had gone on long enough.

"Thank you for bringing it to my attention," she said primly.

"I thought you'd know what to do," he said.

"I'm not sure what that is," said Erica, "but the journal should be returned to the library. Put it back where you found it," she said, handing him the ravaged periodical, minus the remaining page.

"All right," said Ned, reaching down for the buttons on his shirt, his disappointment showing.

"Ned, do you have to wear the book back to the library?"

"Yes, I do," he said. "They check bags on the way in now."

"Well, maybe you could do that in the men's room."

"Okay," said Ned, clearly dejected.

"Do you plan to discuss this with anyone?" asked Erica.

"Not anymore," he said.

"That's probably best," said Erica to no one in particular. The door had already closed behind him.

Chapter Fifteen

Who is that father of any son that any son should love
him or any son?
–James Joyce, *Ulysses*

Erica sat at her desk, head in hand, leaning over the
exam book that currently had her attention. It was the
last week of the semester, when tests were taken and
grades returned in a matter of days.

Erica groaned.

Sarah had chosen this moment to drop in, taking a
break from her own grading. "Are you all right?" she
asked with some concern.

"Sarah, yes. Do you have a minute? I hate to in-
flict undergraduate writing on someone who has more
than enough to read, but I'd appreciate a second opinion."

"I'd be happy to be of help," said Sarah, who took
the book from Erica, seated herself, and read.

"Fences" is a social problem play that was developing during the play itself. Everyone was lied to, etc. No one knew what was going to happen next. It seems according to the play "Fences" that the whole cast (people in the play) wait until something happens before they become aware of it. While trying to talk with each other to find out how it happened. The three categories in the social problem play according to the play "Fences" is 1) lack of communications; 2) awarelessness; 3) misleading information. It seems that according to the play the people who were in charge of the kingdom became sinners within their own rights. After the father's death, he who was king, the son never became king or followed in his father's footsteps. Hamlet became a sinner who also did something to his father's wife. While doing so, he killed someone who was spying on them (Hamlet and the father's wife). Hamlet never became king in this play. There were many social problems that in the long run will effect the whole family. Upon making someone a king of the kingdom, he was lied to. He never knew his mother until he slept with her. Also he later took his eyes out because he didn't want to see the sins around him as long as he lives.

"Is this in code?" Sarah asked.

"Nope," said Erica. "Try again."

"Is English his first language?" Sarah asked.

"Is Earth his home planet?" Erica answered.

"What was the original question?"

"If memory serves, I asked something about August

Wilson's *Fences* in the context of the social problem play. *Fences* is about an African-American family, in Pittsburgh, in the fifties. The father's a garbage collector, the son wants to go to college on an athletic scholarship. Dad won't sign the permission papers—"

"I get the idea," said Sarah.

"This student's answer takes a side trip by way of *Hamlet* and *Oedipus Rex*, which—minor detail—were not on the test. Those plays were on the midterm. I guess he finally got around to reading them, and wanted credit for the accomplishment."

"How did he do on the midterm?"

"How do you think he did on the midterm?"

"Well, your course seems clear."

"Yes," said Erica, "he fails. What is really scary is that this student did not miss one single class. He was always there, seemingly engaged in the process—no glazed expression, regular eye contact."

"Very encouraging signs," said Sarah.

"So how is it possible for him to be in the same room with all the people who passed the course, some who even did well, and not take something in?"

"Did you ever talk to him?" Sarah asked.

"Oh, yes. He's a very nice person. Earthling and English speaker . . . well, more or less. His work is usually a little better than this. He must have felt panicked. Although, I will admit, he doesn't work too hard in school; he saves that effort for the forty hours he puts in each week to make the money to stay here, to produce work like this exam. He really doesn't want to be in school, but he needs that diploma to be considered for a better job. He hoped to scrape by with a D in my class, which ain't gonna happen."

"You win some, you lose some," said Sarah. "It's not your fault."

"I wasn't trying to assign blame," said Erica. "I just wonder sometimes about the point of the exercise."

"Don't. It doesn't help. And everyone's answers are different." Sarah smoothed a non-existent wrinkle on her skirt. "Let's change the subject. Do you have plans for the holidays? Seeing family?"

"They're kind of scattered," Erica began.

"Oh. Well, you know you're welcome to join us—"

"No, but thank you," said Erica, having no desire to play the orphan at Sarah's Christmas pageant. "I expect to be out of town. Seeing friends."

His film career still under negotiation, Alan had long since returned to London for a bittersweet re-union with his understudy. With London a little out of her price range, Erica planned to disappear to New York for a few weeks, hoping to find cheer if she could not spread it.

"Another time," said Sarah, as she rose from the chair, "and thank you for sharing that exam. Suddenly, my own students don't look quite as bad."

"Any time," said Erica. "Feel free to return the favor if you come across a classic of your own."

"I don't think mine would measure up," said Sarah.

"Don't underestimate yourself—or them."

"I don't," said Sarah. "I never have. But wait a minute. I think I *do* have one that you might enjoy."

Sarah left the room briefly and returned with an exam book of her own.

"Why do they still call these things *bluebooks*," said Erica, "when they come in a range of fashion colors?"

"I have no clue," said Sarah. "But try this one on for

size. In the sophomore survey, we're reading Faulkner's 'A Rose for Emily.' "

"Doesn't everyone?" asked Erica.

"And this passage just jumped out at me."

Erica read from the blue book that Sarah handed her. "Poor Miss Emily's fate is loneliness. This is because of her father's strict rules of no sex before marriage, death, and taxes—which she still lives by."

"As my father always believed," added Sarah, "no sex before taxes."

"Words to live by," said Erica.

"Emily apparently does," said Sarah.

"Okay, we're even," Erica conceded. "More or less."

"Yes, onward," said Sarah, as she sailed out of the room.

Chapter Sixteen

Our race would not have gotten far
Had we not learned to bluff it out
And look more certain than we are
Of what our motion is about.
　　　　　　　–W. H. Auden

Later that afternoon, Erica handed in her grades to a skeptical Letticia Franklin.

"More *B*'s than usual," said Letticia, scanning the grade sheet.

"Innumerable," said Erica, backing away lest her phone messages disappear for another few months. She had one more task to fulfill before the semester ended, and she wanted to complete it before good sense got the better of her.

Standing on the stone-cut steps of Brixton's Police Department, Erica hesitated, reminding herself that only in detective novels were people ready and willing to talk to those in need of answers. Erica was also in need of the questions.

The desk sergeant sat across from her, engrossed in his reading. No amount of throat clearing could get him to look up from his battered issue of *Solider of Fortune*. While she waited, Erica amused herself by tracing with her eyes the outline of a bald spot that his crew cut did nothing to hide. Finally, the sergeant glanced up. A smile broke across his weather-beaten face.

"I bet I know what you're here for," he said.

"You do?" asked Erica.

"Professor Duncan?" asked a voice behind her.

Turning to the speaker, Erica offered a tenative "Yes?"

"Professor Duncan, it's Officer Mike—from the night class."

"Officer Mike, of course. How are you?" Erica said with relief. A twenty-year veteran of the force, Mike Fiorucci had been a student of Erica's. At the first class meeting, he introduced himself as "Officer Mike," the way he did during his years as the nice policeman who visited classrooms and gently warned school children about the bad people in the world. The name stuck. Like many returning students, Officer Mike chose his courses according to what fit into an already full schedule. In Erica's class, he discovered a liking for poetry. His paper on Tennyson's "Ulysses" was one that both teacher and student remembered with pleasure. For Officer Mike, the poem offered words to live by: "To strive, to seek, to find, and not to yield."

"She's not here about the job," Officer Mike said to the desk sergeant, who had already returned to his reading.

"Job?" said Erica.

"We're hiring a civilian clerk," he said.

"Oh."

"Why are you here?" asked Officer Mike. "You weren't mugged, were you?"

"Mugged?" she echoed. "In beautiful downtown Brixton?"

"It happens," he said. "Are you all right?"

"Yes," said Erica, trying to mean it. She knew she had to do better than monosyllables if this interview had any chance of succeeding. "Is there somewhere we could talk?"

"I was just signing out for the day," said Officer Mike. "Can I buy you a cup of coffee?"

"Absolutely," said Erica.

In a nearby coffee shop, Erica focused her attention on the waitress pouring a late-day brew into a chipped cup. Officer Mike sat across from Erica, his silence doing little to build her confidence.

"Officer Mike . . ." she began.

"Professor Duncan, it's good to see you," he said. "You know, I really enjoyed your course."

"I enjoyed having you there."

"I still have that paper on 'Ulysses,' " he said.

"I still remember it," she said.

"Are you teaching anything else at night?" Officer Mike asked.

"Not in the near future," Erica answered. "They are keeping me pretty busy during the day."

"That's too bad," he said, then sipped some of his coffee. "Why were you at the station? Is there a problem? I don't fix tickets, but—"

"That wouldn't be a problem," said Erica. "I don't have a car."

"Okay," he said, drawing out the word.

Erica took a deep breath. "You might remember that there was a death in the English Department a few months ago."

"Professor Parkinson."

"You knew him?"

"Yup."

"As a student."

"Yup."

Now Officer Mike was reduced to monosyllables. Parkinson seemed to have that effect on people.

"And?"

"Not to speak ill of the dead," said the policeman, "but it was not pretty."

"His death?"

"No, I mean his class. You come in after working all day, you want someone who's going to keep you interested, or at least awake. Parkinson didn't get the job done. To give him the benefit of the doubt, I think he was trying. We read about some pilgrimage in the Middle Ages, and all he talked about was how it was like packing the station wagon and driving cross country."

"He used to say that a lot," said Erica. "We're still not sure what it means."

"You want to know about his death. That was not a pretty picture either." Officer Mike sipped a little more of his coffee. "That dictionary did quite a job on him—cracked clear through to—sorry, Professor Duncan. I don't mean to upset you."

"Oh, no. It's not me, really. I mean, I'm not the one who's upset—but a number of people in the Department have been troubled by his death." Erica paused, took a deep breath, then continued to lie. "As someone was saying just the other day, it would give us some sense of closure if we had a better idea of what happened." She was lying to someone she liked and respected, someone who liked and respected her. She decided to stop.

Officer Mike's face telegraphed his concern, though his eyes narrowed when he asked, "What are they saying over there? What do people think?"

"Think? They don't think anything," Erica said. "They just wonder a lot," she hastily answered.

"I wish I had that kind of free time," said Officer Mike.

The two eyed each other for a moment.

"You understand that anything I say would have to be off the record."

"Of course," said Erica.

"I wasn't part of the initial investigation, but word gets around. It was pretty routine."

"You must lead an exciting life, Officer Mike. I mean, a dictionary landed on his head."

"Routine in terms of the case," he replied. "Something heavy lands on your head, it's going to be bad for the head—but nothing to raise suspicion. Unless you—"

"That's what I've been trying to tell them, that there's nothing to know," Erica said.

"Isn't that what you folks do? Know things?" asked Officer Mike.

"That's a big part of the job description," said Erica. She added, "I realize this is none of my, I mean, *our,* business."

"You can put your—*their*—mind to rest," he said. "It was an accident, pure and simple. No question of an inquest or an autopsy for that matter. It was pretty clear how he died."

"That's what I tried to tell them," Erica repeated, "but you know academics. They need to complicate things."

"You never did," said Officer Mike. "That's what I always liked about your course."

Erica was not sure how much longer she could rely on his kindness or the general expectation of eccentricity in academics, even the seemingly normal ones. It was time for this to be over.

"Oh, is that the time?" Erica made a grand gesture of looking at her watch. "I'm sorry, but I must go. I need to get these grades turned in," she said, indicating in the direction of her empty briefcase.

"That's okay. I should be going too," said Officer Mike, as he picked up the check and left a tip. "Great to see you again."

"You too," Erica agreed, telling the truth for a change. "I hope you won't think the worse of me for asking about Professor Parkinson."

"Forget it," said Officer Mike.

"Thanks," said Erica.

"No, I mean it," he said. "Forget it."

"Gone and forgotten," she said. "Gone and forgotten."

Chapter Seventeen

The history of the world, my sweet,
Is who gets eaten and who gets to eat.
–Stephen Sondheim, *Sweeney Todd*

Three times was the charm; three strikes and you're out. Erica didn't need a third cliché to get the point. Jamie, Alan, and Officer Mike, each in his fashion, had told her that an interest in Parkinson's death was misplaced, mistimed, mistaken. She would give it and a rest, she would give herself a rest. From the coffee shop, Erica went back to her apartment, packed a bag, and headed for the train station. She needed a change of scene, though Christmas in Alan's empty apartment was a silent night indeed. Bolstered by a few transAtlantic phone calls, she had resolved by New Year's to live a blameless life evermore.

Erica's revels and reverie were ended by a summons from the Department. Checking her phone messages one morning, she was surprised to learn that she had been invited to a Departmental dinner for a potential hire. The late-December interviews at the Modern Language Association, the site of mass hiring and hysteria, must have gone well for someone. It was only January, early days for a job that would begin in September, and already the Department had invited someone to campus for wining, dining, and interrogation.

Erica guessed that she had been included for display purposes, assuming, rightly, that the candidate was a young woman. To show that Brixton was no patriarchy, the hiring committee had varied the menu of more-than-middle-aged white male faces by inviting Erica to sit at the table. As a last-minute hire, Erica had been spared these festivities, so she went with the idea that, in addition to a free meal, the experience would be educational. She had forgotten that there is no such thing as a free lunch—or dinner.

Of those in attendance, Elaine was trying to make the candidate feel at home in a roomful of strangers more interested in the wine list than in the feminism of Christine de Pisan, specifically the *Book of the City of Ladies*, which was the topic of her newly completed dissertation. No Sarah in sight, but Erica expected that the holidays were sacred around the Tillney household. Jamie was in attendance, hanging on every word of Curtis Greenspan, who luckily had two elbows, for Raymond Pieterese also seemed to subscribe to the philosophy of intently looking up at the most powerful person in the room. Greenspan's early retirement package was still under negotiation, but his would-be successors were ever vigilant.

Professors Grayson-Grossman and Leventhal were there, looking mostly at each other. Everyone else looked at the candidate, who managed only a few bites of food between questions. Leah Shapiro was a bright, young woman with good degrees and no better prospects, given the limited job opportunities in her field. At her interview, the committee had covered the questions asked of enterprising medievalists. Satisfied about her fitness to teach, the committee was not supposed to inquire about personal matters, but Leah cheerfully volunteered the information that her husband—she admitted to having one—was a ceramic engineer. A tense moment followed, when no one wanted to admit ignorance of this profession. Leah added that he was willing to relocate. Everyone breathed a sigh of relief and turned their attention to the entrees. All, that is, except Jamie, who managed to tear his gaze from Curtis long enough to acknowledge Erica, at the far end of the table, with a slight nod. She immediately returned it.

Mark Gorman joined them as they moved to dessert, though to anoint or to smear the candidate was unclear. He seated himself in the empty chair next to John Crandall and ordered something flaming. Looking distinctly uncomfortable throughout the meal, John had eaten little, hungrily watching as Leah performed for her future colleagues. His obvious discomfort puzzled Erica, who had assumed that with Parkinson gone, John automatically moved up a notch in the Departmental hierarchy. Perhaps John was simply wary of all new comers. In any case, he listened intently to Leah's conversation, showing particular interest in her praise of Parkinson's groundbreaking article, a reference that earned only a muffled response from the rest of the diners. They quickly passed over the compliment in favor of the liqueurs.

Erica chose this moment to visit the ladies' room, needing a moment of solitude more than another drink. Though women were no longer expected to make these trips in pairs, she was joined by Natalie Grayson-Grossman. Erica put a comb through her hair, slowly, so that she could delay her return to the table, while Natalie offered a few opinions.

"What do you think of her, Erica?"

"She's fine, Natalie, more than fine."

"In, and she knows it," said Natalie. "Personally, I don't care. We don't teach the same century, and I'll have tenure before she has time to turn around. Then she can worry about me."

This was a side of Dr. Grayson-Grossman not generally available to the public. Erica had rarely seen Natalie out of Stewart's protective custody, though she doubted he had been exposed to this facet of her personality.

"And those blond streaks in her hair. Do you think she does them herself?"

Erica shrugged. "I'd have no way of knowing, Natalie."

"Well, if she doesn't, her hairdresser has a fool for a client."

Erica held the door for her colleague as they left the ladies' room. "After you," she said to Natalie. *So I can watch for knives,* she said to herself.

By the time they returned to the table, the quick sips had been taken, and the bill was being settled by the chairman. While the others made their way out of the restaurant, Mark Gorman stayed behind with Curtis, to argue about the tip or the candidate or both. Jamie had taken it upon himself to shepherd Leah in the direction of the parking lot, offering a ride that she gratefully accepted. Answering the same questions for hours on end can take its toll. But Leah has acquitted herself well and would soon be made an offer she would know better than to refuse.

The group stood together at the entrance of the restaurant, waiting for the parking attendant to return, deciding who should ride with whom.

"Erica, can I give you a lift? I'm taking Leah back to her bed and breakfast. Not far from you, if I'm not mistaken."

"Thank you, Jamie, I'm going with Elaine," Erica replied. A look of surprise flickered in Elaine's eyes, but she quickly joined in the spirit of the game.

"Yes, we had so little time to chat this evening. You must come with me," said Elaine, offering the invitation that had already been accepted.

Curtis and Mark had yet to emerge from the dining room, so the clearly dejected Pieterese attached himself to Leah and Jamie. Professors Crandall, Leventhal, and Grayson-Grossman retired from the scene, though together or separately, no one noticed.

The parking attendant was still unaccounted for. Wandering away from the group, Erica wondered if he had parked the cars in the outer reaches of Brixton or simply forgotten where he put them.

"Erica, look out!"

Foolishly thinking herself safe on the sidewalk, Erica looked up to see a small gray car moving with great speed in her direction. At the last minute it swerved, missing Erica and several parked cars before exiting the parking lot. The proverbial deer in the headlights,

Erica was pulled to safety by Jamie, who seemed more shaken than she was.

"Are you all right?" asked Jamie.

"I'm fine," said Erica, haltingly. "What was that?"

"People should really be more careful in parking lots," said Elaine. "That car was heading straight for you."

"Luckily, it seemed to change its mind at the last minute," said Erica. "Anyone we know?"

The group shook their heads in unison.

"What kind of car was it?" asked Jamie.

"My knowledge of motor vehicles is limited," said Leah.

"Don't worry," said Erica. "It's not on the test."

"Some kind of economy model," volunteered Elaine. "Did anyone get a license plate? Erica, are you sure you're all right?"

"Truly," said Erica. "There's not a scratch on me, thanks to Jamie," she said, finally forced to face him. "Really, the excitement's over."

Unfortunately, it was not.

As the group shivered in the cold January air, a heated debate could be heard, coming from the foyer of the restaurant.

"She's a lock, and that's all there is to it," said Curtis.

"I don't question her credentials," said Mark, as he swung open the door to the restaurant, nearly hitting Raymond in the process. "She'll do, but that young man was just too pretty not to hire."

The chairman and his senior colleague suddenly found themselves face to face with their fellow diners.

"God, Mark, you're an idiot," said Curtis, who made a few conciliatory noises to Leah before disappearing into the night.

Erica looked at Leah. "Welcome to the Department," she said.

"Thank you," Leah replied, looking a little dazed, but otherwise undaunted.

Gorman was right, thought Erica. *She'll do.*

Chapter Eighteen

This was a real nice clambake.
We're might glad we came.
The vittles we et were good, you bet,
The company was the same.
–Oscar Hammerstein II, *Carousel*

Erica tried to keep her eyes off the road when she rode with Elaine, who emphasized speed over accuracy. Then again, Erica was not along primarily for the ride.

"Can we do it again real, real soon?" asked Erica.

"Oh, not so bad an evening, all in all. Except for Mark's unfortunate comment and one bad driver, I think things went rather well," said Elaine as she executed a left turn from the right lane.

"That was an example of 'not so bad?'"

"Yes," said Elaine. "As far as Mark is concerned, he usually keeps his feelings to himself, and he would never have said what he did if he knew we were in earshot."

"That makes it okay then?"

"When you've been in this profession as long as I have, you've heard enough inappropriate remarks to last you a lifetime."

"On the receiving end?" said Erica.

"Often enough," said Elaine. "When I was fairly new to Brixton, a senior faculty member, male, of course, said, well within my hearing, '*That one* looks fertile.'"

"He didn't want to plant anything, did he?"

"No," said Elaine, quickly dismissing the suggestion. "It was a sidebar to one of his favorite topics, something along the lines of 'They want tenure, but they keep having babies.' I wasn't even pregnant at the time."

The women of Brixton owed a lot to Elaine, who pioneered the concept of maternity leave at the university, while mothering a brood of her own.

"Those confused ideas fade with time," Elaine continued, "once the boys get used to your being there—"

"Once they see you as one of the boys," finished Erica.

"I hold to the belief that women can do better than merely being boys, or men, for that matter," said Elaine, "but I have no objection to having what they have, or doing what they do."

"Anything they can do, you can do better."

"I can do it as well," said Elaine and "and better than some."

"Then why don't you take over?"

"I prefer to roam the corridors of power, working behind the scenes—"

"Doing that voodoo that you do so well."

"Getting things done in my own way, reminding the boys that we are here to stay—this has dawned on a few of them," said Elaine. "Jamie, for one."

"Yes, our Jamie is a regular feminist," said Erica.

"He speaks highly of you, Erica."

"He is too kind."

"Why did you turn down his offer of a ride?" asked Elaine. "Not that I don't enjoy your company."

"No reason," said Erica lightly. "I expect he wanted me along for appearances. Another woman in the car for the sake of propriety."

"Propriety is very important to Jamie."

"He won Pieterese instead. They can vie with each other all the way home."

"Men and their hierarchies, and poor Leah has to watch," sighed Elaine.

"Poor Leah," said Erica. "She has had a busy day."

"She'll get what she wants out of it."

"And that is?"

"A job in a virtually impossible market. We would all do well to remember that," said Elaine. "Especially those of us without tenure."

"Particularly those of us not even on a tenure line," said Erica, "and yes, Mother—I mean, Mentor—I hear you."

"Do you, Erica? Do you really?"

The question surprised Erica.

"Really and truly, Elaine. I hear you."

"So you would like to stay on, if the opportunity arose."

"I haven't given it too much thought, but yes," said Erica. "Of course."

"Well, my dear, if that is the case, you might act as though that is what you want. You might behave as if you belong. Admittedly, some members of the faculty have difficulty reading the signs, any signs, but you are a bit of a puzzle even to those of us who know you best."

"I think I'm getting the picture," Erica said.

"I hope so," said Elaine. "We'd like to keep you, but we can't if you make that difficult for us."

"Have I been difficult?" Erica asked.

"Not difficult, exactly, just a little hard to pin down."

"Should I feel like the butterfly pinned to the entomologist's display chart?"

"Those butterflies are long gone, and you are still here, alive and wriggling."

"A charming comparison," said Erica.

"You started it," said Elaine.

For the moment, the subject seemed to be closed as Elaine concentrated on her driving, after nearly hitting two pedestrians, who, well within their rights, had expected a safe passage via the crosswalk. Erica winced and tried to take the conversation in a different direction.

"Elaine, you once said that there had been some bad evenings in the Department—on the social calendar, I mean. Any horror stories come to mind? You already told me about Parkinson's unspecified remarks to Dr. Grayson-Grossman."

"Parkinson, yes. I had thought that with his passing we might be spared further embarrassment. So good of Mark to jump into the breach."

"As it were."

"There once was a young man from Yale—"

"Sounds like the beginning of a limerick," said Erica.

"It could have turned into one. Or worse, it could have turned into a law suit. It seems that during one campus visit, the dearly departed Professor Parkinson made some comments to a job candidate that might have be construed as . . . unfortunate. As luck would have it, the young man wasn't interested in making his name as the victim of harassment."

"He had his pride. What did Parkinson say? Did he do something?"

"No, it was just a misunderstanding. He could sometimes be a bit of a bother to boys and girls and the occasional small animal, the ones not fast enough on their feet—an equal opportunity offender."

Erica thought for a moment before asking, "Then why did you bring him on these outings if you knew there was a good chance he would, shall we say, make a nuisance of himself?"

"Erica, he did discriminate. I'm not saying he made advances on every potential hire. Now and again, though, he would say something, not actually do anything, but say something—"

"*Unspeakable*, according to Grayson-Grossman."

"I think it was more of a test with him, a show of power," said Elaine.

"And maybe a tad sadistic?"

"There you have it. As to why we couldn't leave him at home, well, Erica, you may be able to lock the madwoman in the attic, but not the tenured full professor. He is free to wander loose, with a standing invitation to all Departmental dinners."

"What fun," said Erica. "Sorry I missed it."

Elaine took her eyes off the road and looked skeptically at Erica.

"I mean as a spectator, not the recipient of his attentions. I don't know what I mean," Erica said, shaking her head.

Elaine returned her attention to the road. "That's all right," she said. "Parkinson has baffled us all. That last article he wrote is a more recent example. Apparently, he had something to say, after all."

"You've read it?" asked Erica.

"No, it's not high on my list. Should it be?"

"Don't ask me," said Erica. "All I know is that Parkinson may be gone, but we have Mark Gorman to hasten Curtis' retirement. Judging by tonight's performance, Mark wants Curtis out immediately."

"Curtis and Mark have an abiding respect for one another," said Elaine.

"Maybe somebody should tell them."

"Things a bit redder in tooth and claw than you expected?" asked the older woman.

"Not really," said her young friend. "I had some idea of what I was getting into, and what Curtis is getting out of. His must be the longest negotiated retirement in history. Why is he bothering?"

"Why retire?"

"Why retire at reduced pay when some people still teaching have retired at full?" Erica asked.

"We've all heard that joke," said Elaine. "Curtis would not stay around simply to cash his paycheck and mark time in his classes."

"My particular favorites," said Erica, "are the folks who have not reread the material they're teaching in the last, say, ten, twenty, thirty years—"

"One assumes they read it in the first place," said Elaine.

Erica continued. "They stand up at the front of the class and—"

"Reminisce," finished Elaine.

"So you know what I'm talking about," said Erica.

"I've heard tell," sighed Elaine, "but Curtis is an honorable man."

"That's good to know," said Erica.

"Here we are," Elaine said, as she pulled up in front of Erica's apartment building, in the vicinity of the curb. "Home again, home again."

"Jiggity, jig," Erica finished. "Thanks for the ride, Elaine. I know it took you a little out of your way."

"How do you plan to spend the rest of the break?" asked Elaine.

"I think it's time to take a look at my dissertation. See if I can cannibalize it."

"Excuse me?"

"I'll send some chapters out, see if I can get them published as articles."

"Good for you. It's never too early to publish. Too bad John Crandall hasn't done the same. We expected big things from him, but so far, there's nothing in print."

"And that's all that really matters."

"Not *all*, but it matters," said Elaine firmly.

"That might explain some of the lean and hungry looks he was giving Leah during the dinner," said Erica.

"Was he?" replied Elaine. "I didn't notice." Elaine turned over the ignition, although the car was still running. The engine made an angry noise, which Elaine did not seem to hear. "I'm off then," she said. "Enjoy what's left of the vacation. It's a bit of a haul until the next one."

"Only in academia is two months considered a long haul between vacations."

"It only seems long," said Elaine.

"Thanks again," said Erica, getting out of the car.

"I'll wait until you get inside the building."

"That isn't necessary, Elaine."

"I'll wait anyway. Good night," Elaine said as Erica headed up the path. Given the events of the evening, she did not skip down the lane.

Chapter Nineteen

. . . O now, forever,
Farewell the tranquil mind.
–William Shakespeare, *Othello*

The new semester was supposed to begin slowly. Class lists were checked, reading lists were scanned for the degree of difficulty before a commitment was made and the books purchased. Erica looked out into the sea of faces that would become individuals, but for now remained an undifferentiated mass searching for the meaning of modern drama. She took names.

"Toklien," she said.

"Yes," a male voice answered.

"Amor is your first name?"

"Yes."

"A family name?"

"The family of man. And woman, of course. It means love."

"Okay," Erica said uncertainly.

A few students tittered at the exchange, but most waited silently for their names to be called. Their names were Jennifer and Jason, but they had met enough Seagulls and Serendipitys not to fazed by any appellation. Erica moved down the list.

"Whitmore," she said. "Richard."

"Rich," he said.

"And famous?" she asked, looking into the crowd.

"Huh?" A blank face looked back.

"Never mind. Rich is enough."

Having made it through the class list, Erica was about to begin her description of the course, leading to the all-important "how-you-will-be-graded," when her speech was rudely interrupted by the fire alarm. Speaking above the din, Erica told the class how best to exit the basement classroom in which Letticia invariably placed her, and instructed the students to wait outside the building until someone in the Department gave the all-clear signal. She assumed the alarm to be false, but she had been wrong before.

Outside the building, Erica was joined by Robin and Ned, who had been on their way in when they were greeted by the exiting horde.

"Not a promising start," said Robin. "The pranksters should know better. Fire alarms are a tried-and-true method of disrupting exams, but they're wasted on the first day of class. What are you going to miss? Signing the attendance sheet?"

Ned had returned to his custom of saying nothing and rarely met Erica's eyes, choosing instead to watch the building.

"Maybe this will be a short intermission," said Erica.

"Right," said Robin. "The triumph of hope over experience."

"Shouldn't fire trucks be pulling up any minute now?" asked Erica.

"Yes, that's part of the ritual," said Robin.

"Then, where are they?" Erica asked.

"On their way, I'm sure. Have patience."

"Patience? On the first day of what is laughingly called the spring semester? Jack Frost is still nipping at my nose," said Erica. "That makes it winter in my book. What if we were knee-deep in snow?"

"We're not," said Robin. "It's cool and crisp and—"

"Isn't that smoke?"

Ned, with his usual economy, had asked the pertinent question. A moving trail of smoke billowed from the entrance of the Department, followed by the figure of a man. With one hand Jamie held a handkerchief to his face; with the other he held a wastebasket at arm's length. Once outside the building, he placed the wastebasket carefully on the sidewalk. The source of the conflagration had been located.

"A burning wastebasket?" asked Robin. "That's what this is about?"

"Not quite the burning bush, but it will have to do," said Erica. "Maybe now we can get back into the building."

"Don't hold your breath," said Robin. "If the fire trucks aren't here yet, that means a wait for official word that all is clear—which means I'm going to lunch. Join us?"

"No, thanks," said Erica. "I know my class is a goner, but I think I'll wait around. I can dismiss the few students who haven't already left. That is, if I recognize them."

Erica thought Ned looked faintly relieved that she would not be joining them. Walking toward the Department, she wondered how long it would be before the safety signal was sounded. A few students stood over the smoldering fire. Jamie emerged from the building, holding a coffee pot filled with water, which he poured into the wastebasket. The alarm had been silenced without the assistance of the Brixton Fire Department, which had chosen, apparently, to phone this one in.

"Our hero," said Erica as she approached Jamie. "Where did this come from?" she asked, pointing at the wastebasket.

"It was in the hallway outside our office, Erica."

"Someone dropped a cigarette into it?"

"A more direct approach, it seems. Someone dropped a match."

"Someone deliberately set fire to a wastebasket? Outside our office? Why?"

"I can't be sure," said Jamie, "but it followed a rather unpleasant conversation with a student from last semester. She was of the opinion that I undervalued her contribution to the class. She was lucky to get the grade she did, given her performance on the final."

"Crashed and burned, did she?"

"In a manner of speaking," Jamie said. "We parted, not quite amicably, and she closed the door behind her. Then this was found on our doorstep."

"Volatile child. What do you plan to do?"

"I haven't decided yet."

"Can we get back into the building?" Erica tried to see around Jamie, who blocked her view of the entrance.

"Most people never left."

Jamie spun on his heel and entered the building, followed by Erica. This was their longest conversation in several months, but Erica saw no need to prolong it. Rather than return to her office, she made her way to the mailroom where a trio was talking excitedly. Larry O'Brien appeared to be the most agitated, which was not unusual. Since his tenure troubles, most people tried to avoid conversations with Larry. They found that they were not talking to a person, but to a sustained reaction.

"Everyone will think I did this. They will blame it on me," Larry moaned.

"No, Larry, of course not. No one would think this of you," said Elaine in her best conciliatory tones. She followed Larry out of the mailroom, trying in vain to comfort him.

"He thinks they blame him for the fire?" Erica asked Sarah, who stood nearby.

"The fire? Why would they blame him for that? Keep up, Erica. Have you checked your mail?"

"I was just about to."

"There's one memo of particular interest." Sarah smiled and pointed in the direction of Erica's mail slot.

Erica pulled out the assortment of papers that had accumulated over the break. On the top of the pile, the most recent addition caught her attention. The memo read:

TO: Whom It May Concern
FROM: One Who Knows Better
RE: If I Knew Then What I Know Now
Attention job seekers, I want to share with you what I've learned from my experience on the market. Forget about never letting them see you sweat.

*They want to see you sweat. They love to see you
sweat. What you need to know is:*

*Men, leave the wedding ring at home. Bring an
air of mystery instead. Give them that secret
smile. Let them wonder.*

*Women, they'll welcome you with open arms. You
can file for sexual harassment after you get the job.*

That's all for now. No need to thank me.

"Who? What?" was all Erica could get out.

Elaine reentered the mailroom. "Poor Larry," she
said. "This really is too much. Who could have done
such a thing?"

"I have no idea," said Sarah, obviously enjoying the
latest crisis. "Larry does spring to mind as the perpetra-
tor, but I'm ruling him out. The memo shows a little
more control than he is capable of. These days, he
seems to live at the emotional age of twelve."

"It does have angry white male written all over it,"
said Erica. "The poor dear, whoever he is."

"Yes," agreed Sarah. "The poor darling. It must be so
tough."

"Indeed," said Elaine, almost seriously.

The thought of how hard things must be for educated
white men caused the women to burst spontaneously,
contagiously, into laughter.

Jamie poked his head into the mailroom.

"And what is the cause of all this hilarity?" he asked.

"Our cauldron was delivered," said Erica.

He retreated without comment.

"It could have been written by an angry white man or someone trying to sound that way. You didn't write it, by any chance?" Sarah asked Erica.

"Of course not. Why would I—"

"Just curious. I thought it suggested your sense of fun."

"Thanks for thinking of me, but no, it's not mine," said Erica. "Sarah, who do you really think did this?" Erica asked, more pointedly.

"Just find the likeliest job seeker, which lets me out," said Sarah.

"How many people are on the job market?" asked Elaine. "People tend not to advertise that they're looking around. Or it could be the work of a graduate student."

"Yes, they are a creative bunch," said Erica, considering Robin and Ned as unlikely suspects, but wondering if they knew anything about it.

"What about the fire?" asked Sarah.

"Jamie took care of it. He thinks the culprit is a disgruntled student," said Erica.

"Already?" said Elaine.

"He thinks it's someone from last semester. Things can only get better, right?"

"If you say so, Pollyanna," said Sarah, who offered her own version of a secret smile as she left the room.

"I'd like to think so," said Elaine, following Sarah.

"That makes three of us," said Erica to herself.

Lacking another destination, Erica went to her office and found Jamie at his desk, preparing for class. When he looked up from his work, she thought it an adequate opening.

"Did you read your mail?"

"Yes," he said shortly.

"Did you see the memo?"

"Yes." More irritated this time.

"What do you think?"

"I put it in its rightful place. The circular file," said Jamie.

"Who do you think did it?"

"*Whom,* and I neither know nor care." Jamie paused, then aimed, and fired. "You know, Erica, it's becoming a little tiresome to see you behave as if this were one big garden party, and you the unsuspecting Alice."

Surprised by the force of his comment but checking her anger, Erica asked, "Well, what does that make you? The Mad Hatter? No, that's not it. Of course, the White Rabbit. Aren't you late for something?"

"I am, as a matter of fact," he said, as he looked at his watch and prepared to leave.

"What do you plan to do about the alleged arsonist?"

"I'll check up on my unhappy ex-student, assuming that the gesture was directed at me. Don't forget, this is your office too."

"I like to think I'm as paranoid as the next person—maybe more so, the way this day is going—but no, I don't think it was meant for me."

"Well, we'll see, won't we?"

"That we will," said Erica to Jamie's departing back.

Chapter Twenty

What tellst me of robbing?
–William Shakespeare, *Othello*

Alone with her thoughts, Erica tried to unscramble the assorted critiques that had been laid at her door. *All in a day's work,* she thought, *and the morning not yet over.* The ringing phone diverted her from this train of thought. She reached for the receiver.

"Erica Duncan," she said.

"Oh, Erica," said Letticia on the other end. "I was looking for Jamie."

Hearing her disappointment, Erica replied, as brightly as she could, "You just missed him, Letticia."

"Where is he?" asked Letticia.

"Out getting himself adored," answered Erica.

"What did you say?"

"He's in class, Letticia."

"And where is that?"

How should I know? thought Erica. *You make up the schedule.*

"I don't know," said Erica. "He left no forwarding address." Erica waited for a response, but none came. "Is there something I can help you with?" she added sweetly, certain this was an impossibility.

"We have a student and her parents here in the chairman's office," Letticia began, in a begrudging tone. "She has a question about her grade in Jamie's class. We can't seem to locate his grade book. He must have forgotten to turn it in—an oversight, I'm sure."

Yeah, right.

One of the quainter customs at Brixton University was the rule about grade books. At the end of each semester, faculty members were required to turn in all grade books to the head of their respective departments. This way, should a faculty member disappear into the sunset, the administration would have the grade book to remember him or her by. The thinly disguised ruse kept track of the amount of grading a professor did. As Erica knew, Jamie never turned in his grade book. No one had ever called him on it—until now.

"I don't suppose you know where he keeps it?" Letticia tactfully inquired.

Erica wanted to say that this was a violation of everything she believed. She wanted to say that it was a professor's right to administer grades, a right that should remain unquestioned by Departmental busybodies like the one at the other end of the phone. Was Letticia familiar with the concept of academic freedom?

Instead, she said, "Sure, Letticia, I'll take a look."

Academic freedom be damned. The unsuspecting Alice indeed.

She put down the receiver and went to Jamie's desk, knowing exactly where to look. In his bottom left-hand drawer, where at least one colleague stashed a bottle of Scotch, Jamie kept the accumulated clutter of his profession. Neither Erica nor Jamie locked their desks, though this might be the way to come. She opened the drawer and looked in.

Buried under a pile of books and papers, the corner of a grade book peeked out. Erica reached into the drawer, moving aside a paperback copy of *Richard II*. She lifted a pile of xeroxed pages. Parkinson's name jumped off the first page.

"I wondered where I left this," she said. It was the anthology that Robin had left behind, the one Parkinson assigned to his students. Jamie had borrowed the pages without asking, but Erica was more surprised that he wanted to read them in the first place.

She continued to dig through the pile. The drawer was deceptively deep, but she made her way to the grade book with a minimum of paper cuts. When Erica lifted it up, she noticed a small pile of papers underneath, well hidden and never meant to be found. Again, Parkinson's name was on the first page.

"Oh, no."

Erica held the article that had disappeared from the library's copy of *Chauceriana*. Neatly cut from the journal, it had found its way into Jamie's desk and would soon find its way into hers. She flipped through the pages. The last page was gone. This one would be easy to find. It had been in Erica's possession ever since Ned brought the missing essay to her attention.

After carefully closing Jamie's drawer, she went to her desk and opened the center drawer. Slightly dog-eared, but right where she put it, was the single page that Jamie had missed. She knew him to be too careful a scholar to skip the notes at the end. He must have been interrupted while vandalizing the text, assuming he had done the dirty work himself. The notes were as important as the rest of the article, more so in some cases. They acknowledged the author's sources, giving credit where credit is due.

"I've been meaning to catch up on my reading," said Erica. Suddenly she remembered the person waiting to have a word with her. She grabbed the phone receiver.

"Letticia, are you still there?"

"Yes," said Letticia icily.

"I'm so sorry to keep you waiting. I've searched and searched, but I just can't seem to find the grade book."

"Oh?" said Letticia.

"If you like, I can leave a note for Jamie. I'll have him call you as soon as he gets back."

"Fine," said Letticia, audibly irritated.

"One more thing, while I have you on the phone. I'm curious about the student in the chairman's office."

"Yes?" said Letticia, barely tolerating the question.

"Does she smell of smoke?"

Click went the receiver at Letticia's end.

Chapter Twenty-one

(Enter Guardsman, with Clown bringing in a basket.)
GUARDSMAN
This is the man.
CLEOPATRA
Avoid, and leave him.
(Exit Guardsman.)
–William Shakespeare, *Anthony and Cleopatra*

"Gothic, really."

Late in the afternoon, Erica stood outside the Department next to John Crandall, having come upon him as he stared up at the building. She made it a rule never to interrupt people when they were making casual comments to the universe, though she thought his were directed at something closer to home.

"Lost?" she asked. John looked at her blankly, then returned his gaze to the edifice before them.

"This place is Gothic, really. This place and all it stands for," he said.

126

Erica took another look at the building that, in her worst moments, she had imagined as a pile of rubble.

"Oh, come now. It was built in 1920, complete with all the accoutrements. The elevator, among other things, belongs in a museum. It's a firetrap, maybe, but Gothic?"

John would not be swayed. "It's Gothic, and more than a little grotesque. The spires reach toward heaven, and we direct everyone's attention upward. We try to teach them about what goes on beyond their fingertips. Forget about their reach exceeding their grasp. With all this talk about other worlds, better worlds, we don't see what's going on here."

"I'm not sure what that is," said Erica.

"We fail to see that the spires are decorated with the figures of hell."

There was a pause, so Erica was fairly certain John was finished. She spoke.

"John, a gargoyle is only a glamorized rain spout."

There was no reply. Feeling that she was simply the breath in his monologue, Erica watched John for a moment until someone's laugh jarred her reverie. The laughter had an owner who stood a few feet behind them. Jamie's smile could be a malevolent thing: how chilling a set of evenly aligned teeth can be. Instead of approaching them, he walked away, repeating "Gothic, really," and grinning to himself. John seemed to be in his own world, which was where Erica left him. She too smiled and backed away, patting the section of her briefcase that held her required reading. After an instructive day, it would be an illuminating evening.

"Gothic, really," she said.

Erica decided to walk home, hoping that it would help to clear her mind. As she passed the parking lot nearest to the Department, she saw from a distance a man and a woman climbing into a gray car. He, of the old school manners, held the door for his female rider, as she arranged herself in the passenger seat. After closing her door, the driver walked around the front of the vehicle to his door, seated himself, slammed the door, and sped off. As the couple passed her, too involved in conversation to acknowledge anyone else, Erica recognized the Professors Grayson-Grossman and Leventhal, whose patronage of his younger colleague apparently extended to car service. She also noticed that the gray car Stewart drove was the exact make and model of the one that had nearly hit her on the evening of the Leah Shapiro dinner.

There are a million of those cars on the road, said Erica to herself. *Besides, I don't really know cars. It may only look like the one that almost hit me.*

She turned again at the sound of another engine. Apparently, John Crandall had managed to collect himself, for he too was heading home in his own gray car, exactly like the one driven by Professor Leventhal. He carefully made his way out of the parking lot, not looking left or right, and not seeing Erica.

So they climbed into their little clown cars and drove home from the circus, thought Erica. That would be one interpretation. "There are a million and one of those cars on the road," Erica said, out loud this time. "The long arm of coincidence—that's all."

If only she felt convinced.

Chapter Twenty-two

Alice laughed. "There's no use trying," she said. "One
    can't believe impossible things."
"I daresay you haven't had much practice," said the
Queen. "When I was your age, I always did it for half-
an-hour a day. Why, sometimes I've believed as many
    as six impossible things before breakfast . . ."
    –Lewis Carroll, *Through the Looking Glass*

Reading through Parkinson's article that evening,
Erica learned what she had always known, that the
Middle Ages were no place for her. Still, she couldn't
help but admire the author's success at tying Chaucer to
something topical, or timeless and universal, depending on your view of sadism.

What she found most intriguing was the last page,
the one that had sat in her desk drawer for several
months. On this page, before the list of works cited,
were the notes, dutifully acknowledging the scholarly
contributions of other people in the field. She was not

entirely surprised to learn that medievalists had so much to say on the subject. The last note, though, had a more personal touch. It read: "I wish to thank my own Letticia for her continued support and inspiration." Robin was right. Parkinson had dedicated his last work to Letticia Franklin. Why?

Still wrestling with that question, Erica was in her office the next morning at an unusually early hour. She wanted to return the stolen article to Jamie's desk before he noticed it was gone, though she thought this unlikely, given how deeply it was buried. She knew that he would be in the library all day, searching for the latest bit of information on the man of letters who never left home.

With the article safely stowed, she went to her mailbox and found a crumpled piece of yellow paper, the kind that is filled out in triplicate. The writing was almost illegible, but she could just make out the signature at the bottom. It was hers—a signature she hadn't signed.

"You're here early."

Standing at the threshold of Letticia's office, Erica said, "It happens. Do you have a moment? There's something I wanted to ask you about."

"Yes?"

Entering the office, she stood in front of Letticia's desk. No one offered her a seat.

"It's about this form from the registrar. It dates back to the fall semester, but I just got it."

"The administrative wheels grind slowly," said Letticia with a sigh.

"Yes, they do, but that's not what concerns me. This appears to be a drop form for a student who disappeared from my writing class. I hadn't planned to let him drop the course. There was the small matter of a plagiarized paper. I thought my signature was required, but he managed to drop the course without me."

Erica held out the piece of paper, which Letticia took. Squinting at it, she looked momentarily confused.

"Yes, I remember this," she said. "The student came in, just before the deadline, looking for you. He said that he had tried several times to reach you, but he could never find you during your office hours. When I called your office, you weren't there, but Jamie was. We agreed that I should sign the form for you and initial it—which I did."

"I see that," said Erica, thinking, *I just don't believe it.* "So you two agreed, but no one told me."

"I assumed you'd know as soon as the drop form was processed. I never thought it would take months, or that you would mind."

"Mind?" said Erica.

"It was a judgement call. I do that sort of thing all the time. If you have a problem, I suggest you take it up with the chairman, whose name I have signed any number of times."

"I'm sure you thought you were doing the right thing, Letticia, and you made someone very happy." *Not me,* Erica thought, *but one very lucky plagiarist.*

"You know, you don't get enough credit for all that you do," Erica said, abruptly switching tacks.

Letticia managed, "Thank you, Erica."

"I mean it," said Erica. "You don't get nearly what you deserve." She pushed on. "We should all give credit where credit is due—the way Professor Parkinson did in his last article, thanking you for your continued support. That was a wonderful thing."

Letticia's eyes began to fill with tears.

Don't get soggy on me, thought Erica. *This is hard enough.* "What kind of support did you give him, exactly?"

It was too loaded a question for most people, but Erica had stumbled onto one of Letticia's favorite subjects. The floodgates opened.

"I always typed the final copy of his manuscripts. I've been doing it for years," she said, reaching for the handkerchief in her purse. "It's a service I extend to senior members of the faculty," Letticia added quickly.

In case I was getting any ideas, thought Erica.

"He was one of the most prolific members of the Department," said Letticia. "It was an honor to type for him."

"Without pay, of course."

"Of course." Letticia looked shocked at the suggestion. "I expected no thanks."

Which is exactly what you got, thought Erica. "You must have been pleased when he gave you the last manuscript to type," she said.

Letticia looked at her, wide- and bleary-eyed.

"I didn't type that one," she said. "I knew nothing about it until it appeared in print."

"That must have been a surprise."

"It was," Letticia said, "the best kind." She dabbed her eyes. "People just didn't know him. They had no idea what he was capable of."

"I'm getting some idea," said Erica.

"Is there anything else I can do for you?" asked Letticia, sniffing.

"Not for me," said Erica, adding nonchalantly, "Did

you catch up with Jamie yesterday? I left before he got back to the office."

"We handled the situation without him—another judgement call," said Letticia, regaining her composure, once again her professional self.

Erica wondered if the student and her parents had been sent packing or if a new grade now floated in the administrative stream with Jamie's forged and properly initialed signature.

"I'm sure you did," Erica said as she left the office. "That's what you do."

Chapter Twenty-three

Friends, Romans, countrymen, lend me your ears;
I come to bury Caesar, not to praise him.
The evil that men do lives after them,
The good is oft interred with their bones;
So let it be with Caesar.
–William Shakespeare, *Julius Caesar*

"I have called you together," said Jamie, "on a matter of extreme importance to the Department."

Erica had expected to hear those words, but not from Jamie. Not here, in the Department's comfortable seminar room, a location in which she doubted she would ever teach, given the long list of faculty members ahead of her. Not now, at a committee meeting on a subject cryptically described as "Matters Pending" in the memo requiring her attendance. In addition to Jamie and the indispensable Elaine, a notable group had received the same missive, and they were doing little to hide their puzzlement at what had brought them together on a

drizzly March afternoon. Erica found herself seated
next to Stewart Leventhal, who looked incomplete without the addition of Natalie Grayson-Grossman. John
Crandall made no attempt to converse with Sarah Tilll-
ney on his right or Letticia Franklin on his left, and the
ladies responded in kind. Letticia rarely attended meetings, and no one had asked her to take notes in over
twenty years. She chose instead to knit. Sarah seemed to
be marking time until she could make her excuses and
rescue the twins from today's form of enrichment.
Seated in a corner was Curtis Greenspan, practicing for
that time in the not-so-distant future when his removal
from the Department would be complete.

"I'll get this underway, if you don't mind," Jamie
said to Curtis, who waved, nodded, and abdicated re-
sponsibility.

"The Administration has determined that the loss of
Professor Parkinson should be marked in a meaningful
and more permanent way, especially given his growing
reputation in the field of critical studies—the new
sadism."

"The Administration has heard about the new
sadism?" asked Stewart. "I didn't think their interests
stretched that far."

"A few of them are members," said Mark Gorman as
he entered, unbidden, and seated himself at the table.

"Mark, we weren't expecting you," said Jamie, looking for confirmation to Curtis, who seemed equally
baffled by the new addition to the group. "Will you be
joining us?"

"I'm here," said Mark. "Proceed."

"As I was saying," Jamie continued, betraying only
the faintest annoyance, "the Administration has deter-

mined that an emolument should be created. This would come in the form of a scholarship funded by the Administration, in Parkinson's honor. I have asked all of you here today to determine what the qualifications for this award should be, and possibly, which student or students should benefit."

Now that's a poser, thought Erica. *What would be the qualifications for such an award?*

"If I may be so crass, Jamie, how much is the Administration offering?" asked Elaine.

"Yes, I should have said." Jamie looked into a file folder he had at hand. "Ten-thousand dollars the first year, with a promise to increase that amount on a yearly basis, based upon the state of the endowment."

"So, after the first year, it depends on how well they do in the stock market," said Stewart.

"And how long they remember Parkinson's name," said Mark. "The life expectancy of the new sadism may be limited." John Crandall looked slightly pained at this suggestion, but no more than the other faculty members in attendance.

"In any case, Mark, the Administration is willing to go forward with this, and I don't think we should turn them down," said Jamie.

"An offer we can't refuse?" asked Stewart. "Has it come to that?"

"Why would we want to?" Jamie shot back. "The Department is in no position to tell the Administration to come back later when we have a candidate more to our liking."

"I agree," said Elaine. "We should take advantage of this generous impulse."

"Given Brixton's tuition, ten-thousand dollars will

hardly get one student from Labor Day to Christmas—
and that's if she or he is not a hearty eater and doesn't
mind sleeping on park benches," said Erica.

"Erica, you know that more and more of our students
have to get jobs to pay their expenses. That's ten-
thousand dollars a student or students will not have to
earn at a job that takes time away from study," said
Elaine.

"I think Erica is asking if we should divide it up or
give it to just one student," said Sarah.

Erica looked at Sarah with an expression that read
"I am?"

"What we should be considering is whether we shall
accept this money in the first place," said Mark.

"And why wouldn't we?" asked Curtis, finally rous-
ing himself to respond.

"Curtis, do you really want me to answer that question?" said Mark.

"You will have to, Mark, if you think we're going to
turn down a dime the Administration wants to send our
way," replied Curtis.

The pained expressions had turned to shock as the
usually restrained Professor Greenspan appeared ready
to spring from his seat in the general direction of Professor Gorman's throat, to be followed closely by Letticia, who seemed to have other plans for her knitting
needles.

"Perhaps we should discuss this separately," said
Elaine, "and come up with a list of suggestions."

"That sounds reasonable," said Jamie, trying to re-
tain control of the proceedings.

"I think an airing of our differences on this matter
would save time and perhaps eliminate the necessity of

another meeting," said Mark. "Yes, we could wrap this up in one afternoon. Would you like to join us, Larry?"

"Now the party is complete," said an amused Professor Leventhal as Larry O'Brien ambled in from the hallway.

"I took the liberty of asking Larry to join us—"

"And of joining us yourself—" said Curtis.

"I thought he, more than anyone in recent memory, could best speak to what Parkinson has done for this Department."

"Mark, this is not necessary," said Jamie.

"I think it is," said Mark, "especially with the young folks here. They should know the bullet they dodged. Though one or two have been grazed, I think. Don't look so worried, Ms. Tillney. A bad review from Parkinson is almost a badge of honor. It's worse if he ignores you, isn't it, Mr. Crandall? Well, almost. Isn't that so, Larry?"

From the time he entered the room, Larry had stood in place in front of the door, looking straight ahead, unlike the others in the room, whose looks darted from speaker to speaker. It wasn't Mark's question that impelled him to speak, but a prompting from deeper within.

"Parkinson was a complete—" said Larry.

"Larry—" said Mark in a warning tone.

Not quite the eloquence we expected, thought Erica.

"I know he was the one who ruined my tenure chances."

"The Department's tenure vote is a group decision, one that is not discussed publicly," said Jamie, directing the comment to Mark. "You should not blame one person."

"Always the company man, Jamie," said Larry, finally looking at someone. "I know as well as you do how it went down. We all know it wouldn't have gone that way if it weren't for Parkinson."

Larry's statement was a truth universally acknowledged. Jamie had no answer.

Stewart chose this moment to chime in. "He verbally assaulted more than one person in the Department. He should have been shot."

"Actually, Stewart, he was dictionaried," said Mark, "with much the same result. But I digress. Does anyone have anything to add?"

Elaine did. "We should bear in mind that he is being honored for what he has added to literary criticism," she said.

"Nice try, Elaine, but do you really want to go down that path?" asked Mark.

Letticia was more than willing to.

"You people," she sputtered. "You don't know. You never knew."

"Yes, we did, Letticia," said Mark in a manner that only a full professor could use to the chief Departmental secretary. Having said her piece, Letticia gathered her knitting and left the room, bumping into Larry on the way out. Neither seemed aware of the collision.

At least one person had heard enough.

"Has anyone heard about the new strain of Alzheimer's disease?" asked Erica. "You forget everything except grudges."

"I think that will be enough for today," said Jamie, ignoring Erica's contribution to the discussion.

"Yes," said Elaine, "we have more than enough to think about."

Hastily, the inhabitants gathered themselves and

their belongings. Stewart raced out the door to find his other half, with John Crandall in close pursuit. As she left, Sarah walked slowly by Larry, who remained unmoved. She touched him gently on the shoulder and said, "I hated him too." This woke him from his dream state as did Mark's terse "Larry," a sound that he followed out of the room.

Erica was in need of no postmortem and followed her colleagues out the door. The last thing she heard was a conversation between the remaining trio of Jamie, Elaine, and Curtis, which effectively ended the meeting and the discussion.

"We're taking the money."

"Oh, you bet."

"Absolutely."

Erica caught up with Sarah on her way out of the Department, as Sarah paused briefly to open her umbrella.

"That was fun," said Erica.

"If you say so," Sarah coolly replied. "In fact, you had more than enough to say. That tasteless joke was unwarranted."

"Just playing my part," said Erica. "What did you think of all that?"

"All what?"

"I'm still not clear on what we were doing there in the first place."

"Just playing our part," said Sarah.

"Oh, that I get—the random sampling of faculty, quickly assembled. We call it a committee. The senior faculty makes all the decisions, but the whole Department is represented because members of the junior faculty are in the room. Isn't democracy grand?"

"If you say so."

"None of this strikes you as odd?"

"Odd? How so?" asked Sarah, much too casually.

"Well, one of our colleagues was *dictionaried,* for starters."

"I noted Mark's use of the passive voice," said Sarah.

"Yes, the active voice might suggest that the wounds were self-inflicted," said Erica.

"I really don't have the time or the inclination to concern myself with anything that does not concern me," said Sarah, "and *that* does not concern me."

"What doesn't?"

"Whatever you're hinting at. It will have to wait, though. I'm late for the boys," Sarah said, while adjusting the shoulder strap of her briefcase. "The thing that does concern me is my tenure review next year. If all goes well, the only way I'm leaving the Department is feet first. You might give some consideration to your own plans for the future."

"Sarah, you're right as always," said Erica. "They will not only grant you tenure, but carry you on their shoulders across the campus. Just be careful what you wish for."

"Always."

Sarah smiled and left Erica to her own devices. Unlike her friend, who could give the Boy Scouts lessons in preparedness, Erica had forgotten to bring an umbrella. The Department's LOST & FOUND was always a good source of temporary cover, so Erica walked back into the building and up the two flights to Letticia's office, where, in addition to her many other duties, Letticia presided over the LOST & FOUND. The office was empty, leaving Erica to pick through the box without supervision. Even Letticia must occasionally lapse in her vigilance. The only umbrella she could find was in a shade of pink so shocking she did not wonder that the owner had left it behind. Yet, she preferred this garish creation to getting wet. Shoving the box back to its rightful place in the corner, Erica was about to leave when she heard a voice through the open door of a nearby office.

"Letticia," the voice cooed. "You know how I feel about that." A pause. "No, stop it. Now really."

The male voice sounded tickled. Erica was not as charmed.

"We'll talk about it later. No, I can't. Not now."

Thank heavens for small favors, thought Erica, as she moved in the direction of the still unidentified voice.

"Letticia!" The cooing abruptly shifted to condescension. Erica was uncertain of the speaker but mystified by the listener. Would Letticia allow this tone to be taken to her? On school grounds?

Erica stood across from the open door. A man with his back to her, coat and umbrella by his side, was ready to leave for the day. He was alone in the room, his listener at the other end of the telephone receiver he cradled between his shoulder and his ear. As he reached for a stack of papers, the speaker turned and looked at Erica. He betrayed no surprise at being overheard. Hers was the look of dismay, due not only to the identity of the speaker, but also to the identity of the listener. Or at least, who the listener was not.

Turning away from him in an attempt to mask her embarrassment, Erica saw the figure of Letticia Franklin advancing down the hall. To be in two places at one time was more than even she could manage.

Chapter Twenty-four

The question was,
At whose door must the tragedy be laid?
–Lionel Trilling, "Of This Time, Of That Place"

By the next day, Erica had gathered herself enough
to teach.

"I don't know that it is a question of assigning
blame," said Erica, trying to steer the discussion of Ibsen's *A Doll's House* away from the "men are bad,
women are good" approach to the play that a number of
students in her modern drama class were eager to embrace, usually along gender-specific lines. It was so
much easier than actually thinking.

"Professor Duncan, you said that we should let the
play speak for itself," said Katie Morton. Katie was
never one to shy away from speaking for herself, or to
raise her hand and wait until she was called on, which
Erica really didn't mind. It made for a faster, livelier
discussion. Even the teacher can get bored if things

move at too formal and stately a pace. As for the class, they solemnly watched as these interchanges took place, nodding occasionally, most of them perfectly willing to have Katie speak for them.

"Nora says that a terrible wrong has been done to her, first by her father, then by her husband," said Katie.

"She does, Katie, very true," said Erica, thinking, *I hate it when they listen.*

Erica had no particular clue where she was going with this line of questioning. She had already hit most of the salient points of the play, and today was the day before the midterm. She was simply in the mood to have her students question the words of the play. If only they would question something—anything—with the possible exception of her.

"So what is this terrible wrong that has been done to Nora by her husband Torvald and her father, the two people who are supposed to love her most?" asked Erica. "Amor?"

Clearly, young Mr. Toklien was warming up for a peroration. "Nora says that her husband and her father treated her like a child," he said, "a doll child, a doll wife. They played with her and passed her from one to the other, from father to son-in-law."

"Thank you, Amor," said Erica, deciding to share the wealth. "Anyone else?"

"Nora had no opinions of her own," said a quieter voice coming from the far side of the room, a precinct not often heard from. A blush suffused Maureen Murphy's pale face. "Her father didn't let her have any opinions of her own. Whatever he thought, she thought," said Maureen, adding after a pause, "That's just wrong."

"Yes, thank you, Maureen," said Erica, smiling in

her direction. "Now, think for a minute about the world they all inhabit," said Erica. "It's the end of the nineteenth century. Men like Torvald are expected to supply all the opinions. Wasn't he just playing his role too?"

"Torvald was a pompous ass," said Rich, much to Erica's surprise. She would have thought that he found a kindred spirit in Torvald.

"Torvald is often played as a pompous ass," said Erica, "much older than Nora, closer to a father than a husband, and that's the way he treats her. Though I did see a production of *A Doll's House* that had a Torvald much closer in age to Nora. It was clear that they liked each other a lot." The experienced teacher always knows how to galvanize her students. Now that she had their attention, Erica could move on to other things. "We'll come back to that," said Erica, curtailing her commentary. "Now, let's get back to the play. Was Nora incapable of having opinions of her own?"

Maureen still seemed lost in the wrongness of an overbearing father, so Erica left her to her musings and allowed Katie, who had shown great restraint for a few minutes, to jump into the breach.

"Not according to Act III. She has opinions all over the place—about religion, about her husband, about everything," said Katie. A few members of the class nodded in agreement. "She can definitely think for herself."

"Yes," said Erica. "The Nora of Act III, the one who is in control of herself and comes to the final conversation with Torvald as a fully articulate individual, would seem to have very little in common with the twittering songbird of Act I. The one who had to hide macaroons from her husband because he decides how much sugar intake is allowed."

"Unless it was a big act," said Amor.

"Nora says it *was* an act," said Katie. "She did tricks to entertain Torvald, so he would keep her around."

"Keep her in nice dresses is more like it," said Amor.

"She didn't buy nice dresses," said Katie. "She told Mrs. Linde at the beginning of the play that she bought cheap material so she could pay back the loan to Krogstad."

"Nora told Mrs. Linde that she looked good in everything, even the cheap stuff," said Cammi Blakely, always dressed in designer clothing and finally finding something to interest her. "Nora was a total snob about that."

"Nora does seem to be pretty shallow in the early scene with Mrs. Linde, who is very poor and has come to Nora for help," said Erica. "That's what I mean about the Nora of the beginning and the Nora of the end."

"She hides things from her husband," said Maureen, suddenly back with them. "Besides the macaroons, there's the loan."

"And the fact that she saved her husband's life by taking the loan in the first place," Katie added.

"Forging the signature on the loan, don't you mean. She was a forger and a liar. They totally bought her act," Amor said with a little more vehemence than the point would warrant. "That's not even the worst of it," said Amor, his face darkening. "She left her kids."

Ding.

Oh, no, thought Erica. *Not you too.*

Late in the twentieth century, with the wind of women's liberation at their backs, a few mothers had chosen to follow a dream that family life had forestalled. Following this dream required a departure from the center of family life, where the wisdom of centuries had placed women and expected them to stay. It was not a mass exodus, but enough to cause more than a ripple of resentment. Erica invariably taught a student who found Nora's exit a little too close to life. Fathers could abandon the family scene—and did, on occasion—but mothers could never leave their children, regardless of the reason. They just didn't do such things. Just ask her students.

"I don't think she cares about them," said Amor in a small voice.

"Well, let's look at the evidence of the play," said Erica. "What does Nora say about leaving her children? Then we can decide if we accept her version of the events. Remember that the audience at the time was scandalized by Nora's departure. In fact, an alternate ending was written, performed, then discarded. In this ending, Nora tries to leave but collapses at her children's bedroom door."

"That would pretty much negate all of third act, and maybe the rest of the play," said Katie.

I knew there was a reason why that girl's getting an A, thought Erica.

"So it's back to the play. What reason does Nora come up with to explain her leaving?"

"She says she's unfit," said Amor.

"That's a more contemporary word that Nora might use," said Erica, treading lightly. "Why does she say that she can't take care of her children at this point in her life? How about hearing from someone else?"

"She says that she has to educate herself—no one can do it for her, definitely not Torvald—and she can't teach her own children until she knows something about the world," said Jill Gerard, who usually sat near

Katie, hoping, perhaps, that something would rub off. Today something did.

"Yes, Jill. Good. Anything else?"

"She's even going to decide for herself about religion, and not be told what to think by her pastor," said Katie, who could sit silent no longer.

"She doesn't love Torvald anymore," said Cammi, who tried to put a romance novel gloss on everything she read.

"I still don't buy it," said Amor.

"What don't you buy?" asked Erica.

"Well, just because she says this, we're supposed to applaud her as a heroine for abandoning her children?"

Erica knew she had to handle this one very carefully.

"Amor, even if we can accept Nora's argument that her children are better off without her, it's still hard to reconcile that with the undeniably emotional fact of a mother leaving her children. When Torvald, speaking for society as a whole, reminds her that her first duty is as a wife and a mother, she insists that she has another duty that is equally sacred."

"The duty to herself," said Katie and Maureen separately, but in unison.

"A truly radical idea," said Erica. "One that people, even now, may not entirely accept." She drew breath and continued. "Do we expect Torvald to sacrifice everything, including himself, for his children? Is he first and foremost a husband and father, or is Torvald allowed to be Torvald, a human being, a banker, whatever. Nora wants the same thing, the opportunity to know who she is. In her time and place, that's no small thing. In fact, that's no small thing even today."

"She should have been there," said Amor, "for her kids."

They were no longer talking about a character in a play. At least Amor wasn't. Erica wasn't sure where to go with this, when relief came from an unexpected quarter.

"The evil Nora," said Rich.

"The evil Krogstad," Katie countered.

"The evil Torvald," said Rich, clearly on a roll.

"The evil anybody," said Erica. "Or how about the evil nobody? Even the loan shark Krogstad, the easiest one to pin as a villain, has his own backstory. Disappointed in love, he did a wrong thing for which society views him as morally bankrupt. Thanks to the long arm of coincidence, Krogstad is reunited with his long-lost love, Mrs. Linde, and they will work to build a life together while rehabilitating his shaky reputation. I'm not saying that people should not be held responsible for their actions—oh, sorry about that double negative—but even Krogstad is more complicated that the easy assigning of blame would suggest. Bad Nora, bad Torvald, bad Krogstad—where does that get us? Human beings are more complicated than that. Even the representations of human beings are more complicated than that. Just something to keep in mind before the midterm."

By the concentration of eye contact, Erica knew she has the attention of the whole class. She wasn't sure if it was her speech or the word *midterm* that held them rapt, but she was certain that it would be wise not to overtax their focus. Besides, it was time to go.

"That is all for today," she said. "I've already gone

over what you need to study for the midterm. I'll see you all on Friday."

The class quickly grabbed their books and left, almost as a unit, most of them chatting to each other. Amor's departure was slower, more measured, and when he left, it was without a word to anyone.

Shortly thereafter, Erica sat at her desk, looking down in the direction of the work still to be done. A large pile of papers stared back, but she looked beyond them. In her mind, she made a checklist of the pros and cons of what she was about to do, and it had nothing to do with the grading that still awaited her. First, she took attendance.

Jamie knows. Oh, boy, does he know.

Elaine, of course, Erica continued in her mental inventory. *Who knows what, and how, and when did they know it—well, that's something else.*

Sarah knows, she thought. *I'm willing to lay odds on that. Curtis? Doubtful. Mark Gorman? Probably. Larry O'Brien? He stopped knowing things when they took away his tenure. Unlikely.* Erica paused for a moment in her ruminations. *Let's see. Hmmm. What will I have for dinner? More to the point, what will I take out? Hmmm.* Erica shook her head and returned to the task at hand, her brief rest period ended. *Back to some hard thinking. The Gemini twins? The Professors Grayson-Grossman and Leventhal? Maybe yes, maybe no. Though which is which, I can't be sure. But whatever they know, they know it together.*

And John Crandall? You never can tell about some people, said Erica to herself. *You just never know.*

And the imitable Letticia? She knows everything, thought Erica. *Why not this too?*

These deep thoughts were taking a toll on a mind already battered by too much grading.

I wish Alan were here, thought Erica. *Not to be such a girl about it, but it would be nice to have someone to tell my troubles to. Just a reasonably sane person to confide in. He could be my* choragos, *she thought brightly.*

But that would make me a tragic hero. An honor I dream not of. Not that I'd get there anyway. Poor old Antigone, even with the play named after her, didn't get the official nod as tragic hero. That went to Creon. I should teach that play again. Sometime.

These conversations with myself are becoming frequent. And louder.

So far, they stay inside my head, which is maybe not the best place for them.

Sooner or later, she thought, *they will come out. I hope I don't become one of those people who talk to themselves in public. If I'm going to have a full-blown conversation with myself on a bus, at least let it be interesting.*

Erica shook her head again and looked down at the piles of typed pages that refused to grade themselves. The interior monologue continued.

There really is nothing to worry about. No real concerns about my own sanity. Concerns about theirs maybe. But that's probably none of my business. And a little wear and tear on the psyche is probably a good thing. How strongminded can I be? Should I be? Why won't I let this go? Why can't I just let things be? Why was I born? Why am I living?

Erica shook her head once more, as if this would direct her train of thought. She tried to concentrate on the business at hand. The papers looked no more appealing than they had when she sat down.

Okay, then focus. Right now. On this.

"I give up," she said out loud. There was no one in the hall to hear her. Erica quickly grabbed her books and the unread papers and made a hasty retreat for home.

Safely there, Erica made the phone call that she had been contemplating for a while. Not to Alan. It would be late in London. Certainly not to the police. No, this one would go to Western Union. An email would simply disappear in the void, since Alan still refused all entreaties to get online. A phone call would be too direct, leading to more questions than she could answer. A letter would be too slow. This needed to be said now, in ten words or less. It read: WATSON, COME QUICKLY. I NEED YOU. E. She hoped that Alan would be able to break the code.

Alan's reply the next day was less sure, though quick and to the point. It read: ARE YOU HOLMES OR GRAHAM BELL? BETTER YET, *YOU COME HERE. A.*

Not a bad idea, thought Erica, as she crumbled and discarded his response.

Chapter Twenty-five

CHERBURTYKIN
Ta-ra-ra boom-de-ay, sit on the curb all day.
It doesn't matter! It doesn't matter.
OLGA
If we only know. If we only knew.
–Anton Chekhov, *The Three Sisters*

Erica sat at her desk, sorting through its contents, most of which were finding their way to the wastebasket.

"A little early for spring cleaning, isn't it?"

"Cleanliness is next to godliness, Robin. I'm working my way up."

"May I come in?"

"Of course."

Robin entered the office and seated herself.

"No Ned?"

Robin's reaction made it clear that Erica had said the wrong thing.

"We're not joined at the hip, you know."

"Sorry. It's just that I'm used to seeing you two together."

"Well, you'll be seeing even less of us, or of him, anyway. Ned is leaving."

"He is? Where's he going?"

"Law school."

"No."

"Yes. At that place across the river."

"Really? That's going in style."

"Nothing but the best—Ned has a real knack for multiple-choice tests. He aced the law boards."

"Aced? As in—"

"Another perfect score."

"Did you see this coming?"

"Not really. I thought he was kidding when he started quoting lines from *Superman*. Something about 'truth, justice, and the American way.' After a while, I realized he wasn't joking."

Erica privately speculated on what had provoked Ned's interest in jurisprudence. "When you see him, give him my congratulations."

"If I see him," Robin said. *So Wendy and Peter Pan were calling it quits,* thought Erica. "Where have you been hiding yourself? I haven't seen you in weeks."

"I've been working on something," said Erica, "and catching up on my reading."

"Is it a brilliant literary discovery?"

"That might be overstating it. I just had something I needed to work out." Erica reached into the pile of papers. "By the way, I came across this. It's yours, I think."

Erica indicated the xeroxed pages of Parkinson's articles that she had not returned to the bottom of

Jamie's desk drawer. They had been given to her in the first place. If he noticed they were gone, she'd let him wonder.

"Oh, I remember these—slow death by boredom," said Robin.

"I thought you might want them back," said Erica.

"Why?" Robin asked, fanning herself with the pages. "You know, I feel kind of sorry for Parkinson."

"You do?"

"Yes. He died before he knew what he was."

"What was that, Robin?"

"A sadist, of course."

"You know," said Erica, as she deposited a large pile of papers in the wastebasket. "I think he had some idea."

Shortly after Robin's departure, Erica looked up to see a new face in the doorway. A very new face in fact, one that Erica had never seen before. If this were a Hitchcock film, the woman in the door would be played by Eva Marie Saint or Grace Kelly. This was no undergraduate standing in the door, nor even a graduate student, looking vaguely impatient. This was an adult, resplendent in a white pantsuit covered by a matching white coat. Erica looked up and briefly wondered if she would ever live a life in which a white coat, seemingly mohair, would play a role. Probably when her hair turned that shade of blonde on its own volition.

"Can I help you?" asked Erica, fairly certain this was not going to happen.

"I was just looking for Jamie," the woman answered. "Jamison Bordwell?"

"You have the right place," said Erica. "Unfortunately, he's not here."

There was no discernable reaction from the woman in white.

"Teaching," said Erica, with a little more emphasis. "Was he expecting you?"

"No," said the woman. "I thought I'd surprise him."

Mission almost accomplished, thought Erica. *You surprised one person in this room, even if it was not the one you intended.*

"I'm sorry," said Erica, rising from her chair and walking toward the door. "I'm Erica Duncan, Jamie's . . ."—she hesitated for a moment—"officemate." Erica extended her hand, which the woman shook.

"And you are?"

"Anissa. Anissa Van Weelden."

Of course you are, thought Erica.

"I stopped by to see if Jamie was free for lunch. Apparently, not."

"No, he teaches for most of the afternoon," said Erica. *Which would explain my presence in the room*, she thought. Erica and Jamie continued to play a game of hide and not seek, mutually and tacitly agreeing to avoid each other whenever possible. It had worked thus far.

"I thought I might catch him before he went out," said Anissa.

The academic schedule is flexible, thought Erica, *but it doesn't quite cover canceling class in the unlikely event that a fabulous babe decided she was hungry—though, no doubt, it should.*

"I'd suggest that you wait, but it'll be hours before he returns," said Erica. "Would you like to leave a message?"

"Yes," said Anissa, "would you tell him that Ani came by?"

Erica tried to look her most helpful. "If I'm not here when he gets back,"—*which I won't be*, she thought—"I'll be sure to leave a note."

"Thank you, Erica," said Ani, as she floated out of the doorway she had never relinquished. "It was nice to meet you. I'm so sorry to disturb your work."

"Not at all," said Erica, as she resumed her seat. "For such interruptions, work is made."

"Really," said Ani. "Who said that?"

"That would be me," said Erica, as Ani receded into the distance and the mist of memory.

It's almost worth waiting for Jamie to come back, thought Erica. *Just to see the look on his face when he hears that—*

Through the open door, Erica could hear a pair of shoes striding purposefully down the hall. If it was Ani, she'd had not only a change of heart but a change of shoe size.

Racing back between classes, Jamie entered the room. His surprise to see Erica was evident, but his reaction and greeting were brief as he quickly surveyed the top of his desk for something he seemed to have left behind.

Erica watched him for a moment before saying, "You just missed her."

"Who?" Jamie asked.

"Anissa Van Weelden."

This news stopped him in his tracks.

"Who?" Jamie asked again, almost spitting out the word.

"Anissa Van Weelden. She stopped by to see if you wanted to have lunch," said Erica, trying to appear off-hand, but enjoying this more and more.

"Ani was here?" Jamie asked in a tone of disbelief.

"She was," said Erica. "She seemed really nice."

Wealth and privilege radiated from every pore of Anissa Van Weelden—that is, if she had pores. "Really nice" were words that would never apply to her, a fact that had nothing to do with the degree of politesse she maintained when dealing with those less fortunate than herself. People like Erica, for example. People who worked for a living. Which still did not explain her connection to Jamie, who also drew a paycheck, though perhaps not with Erica's eagerness on payday.

"She's a friend?" asked Erica, giving Jamie her most innocent look.

"Yes," said Jamie, "A friend. She was here?" he repeated, still in disbelief.

"She was," said Erica, once again reminded that the separation of church and state had nothing on the compartmentalization of Jamie's life.

"Don't worry, Jamie, I was very polite. Also, the cleaning lady came last week, so the place was quite presentable." *As was* I, thought Erica.

Jamie had found the missing book, which he clasped tightly in his hand. He had only a few minutes to return to the classroom in which he demanded punctuality. Betrayed by his whitening knuckles, the grip on the textbook became tighter. "I'll call her when I get home."

"Okey dokey," said Erica, as Jamie strode out of the office with a long afternoon ahead of him. Erica considered Jamie's lost opportunity her gain.

"Jamie has a girlfriend, Jamie has a girlfriend," Erica sang quietly. "Anissa Van Weelden," she chuckled to herself. "And good old Jamie. Who knew?"

She knew, thought Erica. And she also knew that Jamie would not like that one bit.

Not bad as days go, thought Erica, smiling as she reached for another paper to grade.

Chapter Twenty-six

Oh, I am fortune's fool.
–William Shakespeare, *Romeo and Juliet*

Erica stood at the open door of John Crandall's office, the afternoon almost in shadow. He sat hunched over his desk in a room lit through venetian blinds, a pattern of bars lining him and the wall he contemplated. Shifting in his seat, he turned his attention to the pile of exam books before him. John looked as if he'd been there forever, or would be, drowning in a sea of unclear antecedents and sentence fragments. Erica had not found the words to tell him what she knew when he looked up and saw her.

"Erica. What a surprise. Come in." He quickly cleared the books and papers from the chair beside his desk, unceremoniously dumping them on the floor. She entered the room, closing the door behind her, and sat down in their place.

"Maybe I do know what this is about," he said. "A

friend of mine at University Microfilms told me that you had requested a copy of my dissertation. It happens so rarely that he thought I'd want to know. I'm flattered."

"You should be. I don't read just anyone's dissertation. I barely made it through my own."

"Then I'm truly honored. The works of Chaucer are a little out of the way for you, aren't they?"

"Usually, yes—but Parkinson's last article got me started. It kind of fell into my hands. I thought I'd come to you, as the ranking medievalist, to help me make sense of it."

"If I can."

"I'd say you're ideally suited."

Erica crossed her legs, trying to simulate the pose of confidence that she did not feel.

"Parkinson was not what you'd call a cutting-edge kind of guy when it came to scholarship," she said. "He wouldn't know a signifier if he fell over it or a sign if it fell over him—but that essay! That was something new and different."

"It has generated a lot of excitement," said John.

"You don't seem too worked up about it."

"Should I be?"

Uncrossing her legs, Erica got up and walked to the window, where she peeked between the venetian blinds. A bend in the river could be seen between buildings.

"Then we have your dissertation. Most of it is the usual academic exercise. You show that you've read the right articles and authors. You know what you're talking about. Now and again, though, you do manage to break free, if only for a moment, to say something that is yours and yours alone. In your case, I mean, of course, the section on *The Wife of Bath's Tale*."

John offered no reaction.

"To find that part I had to read more about Chaucer than I ever wanted to know, but it was far and away the best part of the dissertation, in my humble opinion. It was more than a blueprint for the Parkinson article."

Still no word from John.

"Anyone who knew Parkinson would know that there's no way he wrote that article. We both know that. A few others do too, I suspect, but they seem to have taken a vow of silence. Have you?"

The expression on his face told her that a decision was being made. John looked almost relieved.

"Sooner or later, someone had to notice," he said. "I'm surprised it was you."

"That makes two of us. Feel like talking about it?"

"Erica, Parkinson did not steal my ideas. He was much more thorough and far lazier. He stole the entire article, the one I had been working on for years. I'd been trying to finish it between teaching during the day and in the evening and all summer. I do support a family on an academic salary."

"Yes, I know you do," said Erica. She also knew that John's family had more than a little to do with this, but she let that go for now.

"How did Parkinson get his hands on your article?"

"I gave it to him."

"You *what*?"

"Not to steal. To read. He may have been a pedant, but he was a well-published pedant, and he knew people at the right journals. I thought if he liked it, a few words from him and it would get published. Little did I know that those words would be 'It's mine.' "

"Okay, so you handed him a copy of your article, but you must have other copies."

"Well, actually, no."

"How is that possible? This is the computer age. You must have heard about it. Files saved on disks? Disks saved on back-up disks?"

"I use a typewriter—a manual typewriter, actually."

"So did Parkinson. Is it a thing with you medieval-ists? Why didn't you just write it out in longhand on an illuminated manuscript?"

John had no answer for that one.

"Have you heard of Xerox machines?" Erica contin-ued. "Maybe an old-fashioned guy like you prefers car-bon paper."

"In my haste to get his good opinion, I handed him my only copy."

"He knew that?"

"I think I mentioned it. I asked him to be careful."

"I think it's safe to say he took special care with those pages." She looked at John with disbelief. "Your name was nowhere on the article?"

"Only on the title page, which he ripped off."

"Among other things," said Erica.

"After I handed him the article, I heard nothing for weeks. Finally, I pressed him on it. He said he hadn't had time to read it, and kept putting me off. Then, the fall edition of *Chauceriana* arrived in my mailbox. It was the same day as the Department's cocktail party. I read it to try and stay current with the latest develop-ments in the field. It was then that I discovered *I* was the latest development—my article, with Parkinson's name on it, rushed into print. He didn't change a word, right down to the notes at the end."

"You're assuming he read that far."

"What do you mean?"

"It was the note at the end, the final note, that said it all for me." She recited from memory. " 'I wish to thank my own Letticia for her continued support and inspiration.' I wonder if he knew it was there, and left it in as a private, sick joke."

"I don't get it."

"Letticia Franklin typed the final copy of all of Parkinson's manuscripts except this one. We're supposed to believe that, after all these years, Parkinson suddenly praised the efforts of his trusty amanuensis. I don't think so. I would never accuse him of that kind of thing."

"Instead, you accuse me."

"I accuse you of knowing what your own Letticia has done for you, and continues to do."

John said nothing.

" 'Tish' is a nickname, of course. Few women her age are named Letticia. It's a name that belongs to another generation. Your wife is known as 'Tish' but in the note—and on the phone the other day—you referred to her as 'Letticia.' Why is that?"

"I tease her with it. It's a term of endearment."

"She must have been flattered by the acknowledgement."

"She knew nothing about it. I planned to show it to her when the article was published, but the way things worked out, I thought it best . . ." John trailed off.

"She never saw it?"

"No."

"She never read the article?"

"I need her encouragement more than her editorial comments."

Erica waited for a moment before moving on to her next question.

"John, you could have screamed plagiarism and made a pretty compelling case. Why didn't you? Out of respect for the dead?"

"I thought that was self-evident."

"Would you mind explaining?"

"Yes, I would."

"Okay, let me have a crack at it. Feel free to chime in at any time."

John resumed his silence.

"I have a theory, and it's only a theory, that Parkinson's death was not as accidental as everyone believes. For the sake of argument, let's say that there was just the hint of premeditation. Now, we have to consider the big three: means, motive, and opportunity. The greatest of these is motive."

John showed no reaction.

"Means is a dead certainty. That dictionary flew through the air with the greatest of ease. Opportunity is more wide open. In the late afternoon, only the secretaries are left in the Department, and maybe a few people who teach at night. On the afternoon in question, if you'll recall, even the secretaries had abandoned their posts and were in the Founder's Room, drinking to the greater glory of the Department. Even Parkinson was there, although he must have returned to his office at some point during the festivities. Everyone was coming or going, unless they never showed up at all. It's almost impossible to account for anyone's whereabouts."

John just stared at her, giving nothing away.

"Which brings us to motive," Erica continued. "In the last few months, I have learned that Parkinson managed, in his own quiet way, to offend any number of people in the Department, and he got to you in a big way." She paused. "Feel like sharing?"

"Try and prove any of this," John said.

"Who said anything about proving this? I just want to know what happened."

"As an academic exercise?"

"Yes, to satisfy my intellectual curiosity. When I look at you, am I supposed to see screw-up or conspiracy?"

"When you look at me, you see what you want to see."

"Tell me how he died, John."

"You understand, if the information leaves this room, I'll deny every word," John began.

"I doubt either of us has anything to gain from it," Erica replied.

"I'm glad you feel that way."

Erica resumed her seat as John rose and moved toward the windows.

"I went to the party with the idea of finding Parkinson," he said. "When Tish went off to talk to some of the wives, I made my way over to him. He said he couldn't talk there, to meet him in his office after the party. I wasn't about to make a scene, so I agreed."

"He stayed at the party for a while—just standing there, grinning to himself. I kept to myself, watching him, waiting for him to leave, which he finally did. Tish needed to get home to relieve the babysitter. Time is money, after all. I told her that I had forgotten something in the Department, and sent her on her way.

"When I got to Parkinson's office, the door was open. I walked in and stood at his desk, across from him. I remember it had gotten cold that afternoon, and I was dressed for the outdoors. Coat and gloves, which I never took off. I wasn't there that long."

An image came to her mind of two clips at the end of John's coat sleeves, attached by his wife so he wouldn't lose his mittens.

"I found a man without a care in the world," John said. "Leaning back in his chair, feet up on the desk, legs crossed at the ankles, hands folded behind his head. I threatened to expose him as a thief and a liar. He laughed at me. He said I could do what I wanted, it would be his word against mine. He had a national reputation, and I had none."

"John, if he's known for anything, it's for abject pedantry. That article is unlike anything he's ever published before."

"I've never been published before. Who do you think they would believe?"

"You could point to your dissertation and show that the idea was yours."

"People borrow from graduate students all the time. They're ripe for the picking, and usually grateful for the attention. Besides, my dissertation was only the germ of an idea. The article was a mature working out of the problem."

"For mature audiences only," said Erica.

"You have to get people's attention," said John, returning to his seat. "I needed that essay to save my career. I had no idea the stir that article would cause," he said, almost smiling.

"You must be so proud," said Erica, "but did you have to kill him?"

"I did not kill him, Erica. I may have let him die."

"A distinction without a difference?"

"Not to me."

"Okay. Convince me."

John tried. "The longer we talked, the angrier I got—but he was euphoric. He dared me to expose him, saying that the only career I'd ruin would be my own."

"You were the victim in this, John." She reconsidered her words. "Well, you were . . ."

"The more we argued, the more trapped I felt, powerless to do anything," John said.

"Well, you did do something," said Erica.

"I couldn't stand it anymore. I exploded. Suddenly, my hands were fists."

"You hit him?"

"I hit the desk. I slammed down my fists." He snickered. "The dramatic gesture didn't make much of a noise. My fists were gloved, and I hit the blotter on top of his desk. It did have some effect, though. It caught him off guard, and he fell backwards out of his chair. He reached out to save himself by grabbing the bookstand beside his desk. I don't know why he did that. Instinct, I guess. The stand wasn't secured and neither was the book on top of it. They both fell on top of him, with the dictionary doing the most damage."

"Was he dead?"

"I didn't take a pulse."

"You did *nothing*?"

"I left in a hurry, slamming the door behind me. He

looked dead to me, but my degree is in English Literature, not medicine."

"Was that what you wanted to see?"

"Maybe. When I got to the hallway, I stopped. Needless to say, at that hour, no one was around. I listened at the door. Not a sound. I twisted the knob. The door was locked. It locked automatically when I closed it. They do that, you know."

Yes, they do, thought Erica, remembering her own position.

"An anonymous call to the police might have saved his life," said Erica.

"It would have ended mine," said John. "Parkinson was beyond saving, so I decided to save myself. I walked out of the building and went home."

Erica could say nothing. John had a little to add.

"Parkinson stole the best idea I'll ever have. Yes, Erica, I did have the big three, as you put it. Motive, most of all. I couldn't risk anyone making the connection, not with him bleeding on the floor, but I didn't kill him. You must take my word for that."

"Not to put too fine a point on it, but there's some reckless disregard for human life in there somewhere. Maybe a touch of depraved indifference? Not an act of commission, but—"

"He did it to himself."

"John—"

"He did it to himself."

So much for that line of questioning. Erica could see that they would make no further headway. She rose from her chair.

"Where are you going?" John asked.

"We're done here, aren't we?"

"What do you plan to do?"

"Go home, order Chinese, and grade papers."

"What about—"

"John, I should probably huff and puff and turn you in to the proper authorities—but I'm not sure who'd they be, and, as you so eloquently put it, I couldn't prove this if I wanted to. It's one of those rare moments in higher education when knowledge doesn't benefit any one. So, there's no need to practice your denials. I don't plan to say anything, because there's nothing to say."

"How can I be sure you won't change your mind?"

"You must take my word for that."

John did not look convinced.

"I don't deserve this, you know."

"No one deserves this—not even Parkinson," she said. "Wait," she continued, as another thought occurred to her. "I have one more question."

"Yes?"

"All this talk of dissertations has reminded me of Leah Shapiro and her recent visit to our fair campus."

"She accepted the offer," said John.

"I knew she would," said Erica. "That's not what I'm wondering about. It is customary for a candidate to send in a chapter of the dissertation, about twenty pages or so, for the committee to read. I'm sure Leah did that. Did you?"

"Of course. It was only four years ago."

"Which chapter did you send in?"

"The chapter on *The Wife of Bath's Tale*. It *was* the best part of the dissertation."

"Didn't anybody notice the striking similarity between Parkinson's article and your own work?"

"I don't know what they noticed, Erica. Certainly, no one has mentioned it."

"Who was on the search committee then?"

"Everyone who wanted to be. All the senior people, plus a few junior faculty they drag along. Now, I can't be sure who actually read my work . . ."

"I wish I couldn't," Erica interjected. "Elaine was there, I assume."

"Of course."

"And Gorman?"

"Just try and keep him away. Even Jamie was included, though he didn't have tenure yet."

"Of course he was. What about Parkinson?"

"He would have to be."

"No doubt. Did he say anything about your work?"

"I got the distinct impression he hadn't read it. Which was odd, given that he was a medievalist and would be expected to have an opinion. He offered none. In fact, based on his lack of reaction to me, I didn't think I'd gotten the job. Finally, they made an offer anyway."

"So here you are," said Erica. "Four years is not a very long time, John."

"No, it's not, but I expect that these things blur over time. One search is like another, and one candidate's prose is quickly forgotten."

"John, there are two kinds of people in the world. The people who remember everything, and the people who remember nothing. We work with both kinds of people."

"I know."

"But so far—"

"Nothing."

"Then you're safe, and I've got to go." Preparing to leave, she asked, "Do you want the door open or closed?"

"Closed, please." John regained his composure, and added, "Can I ask you one thing?"

"Of course."

"When you look at me, what do you see?"

A lifer, she thought, but said instead, "I know it can't be easy to play Judas to yourself as Christ."

She left the room, closing the door behind her. With the click of the lock, she walked away.

Chapter Twenty-seven

This is the way the world ends
Not with a bang but with a whimper.
–T. S. Eliot, "The Hollow Men"

Several days had passed since her conversation with John Crandall, and Erica was ready to make an announcement.

"You're leaving?" said Sarah, as Erica caught her up to her in the hallway.

"Yes," said Erica.

"For the day?" asked Sarah.

"For the duration," said Erica.

"So you *were* on the market," said Sarah. "You got another job."

"Not as yet."

"Did you get fired?"

"Fired?" Erica asked. "What makes you think I got fired?"

"Then why would you leave?"

"Let me see," said Erica. "How about irreconcilable differences, maybe even a healthy dose of professional integrity—not to mention a fatal lack of self-interest."

"It sounds like you had a bad day," said Sarah.

"Not great, not terrible," Erica replied.

"Well, you are a great withholder of information."

"No more than some, Sarah. I didn't think you'd want to hear what I have to say."

"Listen, I want to hear all about it. It will have to wait, though. I'm late for the boys," said Sarah. "There is just one thing."

It seems the boys will have to wait after all, thought Erica.

"I've gotten the impression that you think something has been going on in the Department, something of which you are painfully aware, while I am blissfully ignorant," said Sarah. "This could not be further from the truth. In fact, I am insulted by the implicit suggestion that anything that would capture your notice would escape mine."

"No offense intended. I wasn't sure what you knew and when you knew it. We're still dancing around the topic. So, Sarah, spill it."

"Spill what?"

"The truth—details of whatever you think is going on, what I am supposed to know, but suppose that you don't."

"The truth is that Parkinson is dead, but we are way past Parkinson."

"Where are we then?"

"We're at a point where you have to decide. I refuse to believe that you would walk out the door on a whim. Your studied nonchalance has its limits."

"But I studied so hard."

"Yes, you did. It would be a shame to let it all go to waste."

"The nonchalance or the education?"

"Either one."

"Let's get back to Parkinson," said Erica. "The one we are way past."

"No, let's stay with you. Why complicate your life, and possibly *mine,* by pursuing what would have to be a dead end according to the various meanings of the word. You once said you wanted to be just like me when you grow up. Well, grow up."

"If I'm going be to an adult about this, what exactly would you have me do?"

"Erica, if you want to walk away from something, put a far distance between yourself and those activities that do nothing to promote your career. Wondering what might have been is a pointless exercise—be it about Parkinson or anything else."

"Sarah, I don't go through life asking 'How will this affect my tenure review?'"

"Perhaps you should. If I may be so bold—"

"You may."

"You should be more like me."

"A sphinx without a secret?"

"A sphinx with a certain future."

"If I may shift metaphors for a minute here, I'd say you have fallen into the deep end of denial. I just hope you don't drown."

"I'm an excellent swimmer."

"Yes, Sarah, you'll always stay afloat. I'm sorry we didn't get to know each other better—though, now that I think of it, this may be as close as we need to come."

"That may well be."

"So now, it's off to the boys. Give them my best," said Erica.

"You'll think about what I've said?"

"I'll never forget it."

The two parted company, and Erica made her way to Elaine's office. After the limited success of her conversation with Sarah, Erica decided a more civilized approach was in order. She found the eminent Victorian in her office, seated below a framed and signed picture of Tennyson. Her students often asked if Professor Lane knew Tennyson personally. She did have his autograph, after all.

Erica's news did not go over that well.

"You're not *leaving?*"

"So it would seem, Elaine."

"Have you spoken to Jamie? I know he'll have something to say about this."

"Jamie always has something to say. I'm just not sure I'll listen."

"We can't have this. We really can't."

"You haven't asked me why I'm going. I'm sure you know I wasn't fired."

"No, of course not, but we can't let some little unpleasantness derail a promising career."

"Which little unpleasantness do you mean?"

Elaine said nothing.

"The semester is ending, Elaine. We're running out of time. I'm running out of patience—even with you."

"I suppose we could start with Parkinson," said Elaine.

"Could we?" asked Erica.

"All right, then," said Elaine. "All I can say is when a

respected professor suffers an unfortunate death at the time of his greatest professional triumph—"

"Elaine, his eulogy was months ago. I was thinking of something a little closer to the truth."

"Must we?"

"I think we must."

Elaine tried. "I'm speaking only theoretically, but one might be tempted to call into question the authorship of his groundbreaking article—"

"Given its sharp deviation from his earlier work—"

"Followed by the death of the author, a death that might itself be viewed as questionable."

"You're getting warm."

"All right, alleged author."

"Warmer."

"It may be the only explanation that fits the available evidence," said Elaine with a sigh.

"We're literary critics, Elaine. We can make any explanation fit the available evidence."

Elaine went on. "These things can get messy. Luckily, for all concerned, they didn't—no wild accusations, no public embarrassment."

"For the simple reason that no one noticed."

"That's not quite true. You noticed, Erica."

"So did you, and Jamie," said Erica.

"All I'm trying to say is you must let things be. It does not concern you."

"I'm hearing an echo. Sarah said much the same thing."

"You discussed this with Sarah?"

"Again, only theoretically. Suffice it to say she will go to her death disavowing any knowledge of whatever it is we're talking about."

"We can always count on Sarah. What about you?"

"To ignore what's right in front of me? No, I can't do that. To announce my findings to anyone who will listen? No. We have the example of Parkinson before us, proving that it is possible to publish and perish."

"No one's threatening you," Elaine said.

"Not yet—and for now, I'm not threatening anyone. That's the best I can do."

"Why must you leave? It's a waste of teaching talent."

"For me, it's been an education. I now know that even in the ivory tower, the expedient end is the only way to go. The greatest good for the greatest number. The fact that I won't be among that number will be a matter of very little interest for a very short time."

"You have to leave," said Elaine.

"Excuse me?" said Erica.

"You have to leave," said Elaine, "because I have to teach. Talk to Jamie. You may be able to work something out."

"I doubt it," said Erica, "and just one more thing."

"Yes?"

"I think you know how much I have admired you, Elaine. You are a woman of intelligence and intregrity— or at least you passed for one. So how could you, of all people, knowing what you know about Parkinson, do what you did?"

"Erica, I did nothing."

"Exactly."

"Erica, my dear girl—and I do mean *girl*—you too have been passing as a woman of sophistication. These stabs at sleuthing are wasted on Parkinson, but this seems to be less about Parkinson than about you. My dear, decenter the universe. Our little world, the one that does not revolve around you, will manage to survive with or without you. We'd rather you join us, but that would be up to you."

"Are there secret meetings? An official handshake? Will I get a decoder ring?"

"You'll have to stay around to find out."

Erica's decision was immediate.

"Thank you for thinking of me, whatever you're thinking of me. I'm not entirely sure what I'm being offered, but I'll have to say no. Good-bye, Elaine. Knowing you has enlarged my mind."

"Have I?" said Elaine as she beat Erica to the door. "Well, what's a teacher for?"

Chapter Twenty-eight

You know I hate, detest, and can't bear a lie, not because I am straighter than the rest of us, but simply because it appalls me.
–Joseph Conrad, *Heart of Darkness*

Erica stood in Parkinson's office, flipping through the dictionary that had done him in. With the semester almost over, most of the books lining the walls, along with the nastily stained rug, had been removed. This volume remained, however, and looked none the worse for wear. As Erica fingered the pages, the new occupant of the office quietly entered.

"Fancy meeting you here," a familiar voice said.

"Jamie."

"What are you doing?" he asked.

"Admiring your new location. You are moving up in the world."

"I think it will do nicely."

"Nicely? Are you kidding? The halls are alive with

the sound of teeth gnashing. Raymond Pieterese, for one, does not look happy. If they gave you this office, they have big plans for you."

"Your speculation is flattering," said Jamie, obviously pleased.

"Come on, Jamie. What we have here is a sign, in big letters—now we know who's at the head of the class."

"Thank you, Erica."

"Unless a dictionary lands on his head."

Jamie's face registered his distaste for her comment.

"Lest we forget, a man died in this room," said Erica. "This very dictionary dented his brain. He wasn't a very good man, and they weren't very good brains, but he died, all the same."

"That's old news, Erica."

"Yes, the case is closed."

"The case was never opened, except in your fevered imagination."

"You're right, Jamie, and just to prove I'm as much a moral relativist as the next person, I was willing to think that without a crime, there was no culpability. So much for peer pressure. But a crime *was* committed here, and we are all complicit."

Suddenly, Jamie did not look happy.

She continued. "It is laughable to think that a dictionary landed on someone's head, and that it got there without help. We'll let that pass. Chalk it up to a form of justice. Not poetic. Pathetic, maybe. It's more ridiculous to accept that Parkinson wrote his last essay without lots of help."

"All right, Erica. Even a cursory glance at the text—"

"So you did see it, Jamie—"

"I took a look—"

"I know."

Jamie forged ahead. "Even a quick look would indicate that Parkinson could not possibly be the author. He *was* up to screwing with Larry O'Brien's tenure review just because he felt like it. Now that you know about Parkinson, and now that you know that *I* know, does it make you happy?"

"Not really," she said.

"There's still one little problem," Jamie continued. "With no dissenting voices, except possibly yours, one would be hesitant to raise an objection. Someone may be the wronged party here, but he or she, for whatever reason, has kept silent."

"Do you want to know who—and why?" asked Erica.

"No, thank you," Jamie said quickly. "I prefer not to be tainted with that knowledge."

"Too late. I think you already have been."

"That may well be, but I have no desire to recruit problems. I plan to run this place some day."

"Sooner than later, by the looks of it. Curtis has made his final arrangements?" Erica asked.

"Very nearly signed, sealed, and delivered," Jamie answered. "Unlike you, I have no intention of sacrificing the integrity of the Department on some misguided quest. A plagiarism scandal is the last thing we need."

"Not to mention a murder. Don't worry, Jamie. The honor of the Department has been preserved. Turning a blind eye was one thing, but removing the nearest copy of Parkinson's triumph was truly a humanitarian gesture. Were you holding onto it for safekeeping?"

"What are you talking about?"

"You know as well as I do. The destruction of library property was a wasted effort. People weren't exactly beating a path to the reserve room. Parkinson's avid readers, whoever they might be, are keeping their opinions to themselves. A student brought it to my attention."

"A student accuses me?" Jamie asked hotly.

"Relax. No one is accusing you of anything, but you do have the most Pavlovian response to my mentioning Parkinson. The first time, I got an invitation to dinner. The second time, well, I'm not sure what that was about. Attempted seduction is above and beyond the call of duty. Was I supposed to be so overwhelmed that all other thoughts would go right out of my head?"

"I won't dignify that remark."

"No need, Jamie. What will it be this time?"

"You have been reappointed for next year," said Jamie. "That appointment includes a place on the tenure track."

"What's the other option?"

"Your letter should go out this afternoon. I believe Letticia is typing it, even as we speak."

"Now that she has more free time."

Jamie seemed not to hear her. "In case it is of interest to you, Larry O'Brien has received a contract extension. He'll be reconsidered for tenure in three years."

"I didn't know they had those," said Erica.

"We make use of them in special cases."

"So push came to shove."

"What are you talking about?"

"I'm not talking about Parkinson's dictionary, or maybe I am."

Jamie said nothing.

"Gorman must be pleased," said Erica.

"Yes, Mark seems to take a perverse pleasure in keeping us all on our toes."

"I'm sure he does, but let's get back to my appointment. I'm equally sure your fingerprints are all over it. Keeping you friends close and your enemies closer?"

"Are we enemies, Erica?"

"Are we friends, Jamie?"

"You earned this," said Jamie.

"I know I did," said Erica, "but how long can I be trusted? What to do? I know! Let's appoint that potential troublemaker to a tenure-track position where we can keep a close watch on her. She opens her mouth, she loses her job. Or, maybe we can convince her in the intervening years that silence would be best for all concerned. It certainly is best for us."

"I've never thought of you as paranoid," said Jamie.

"Maybe you should. The true definition of a paranoid is someone who sees things that other people miss—and it doesn't have to be little green men—which makes both of us paranoid."

"How interesting. Now, what about the offer?"

"I'm turning it down."

"You have another?"

"I wasn't on the market, Jamie. There are no other offers."

"Erica, you've worked too hard to be so cavalier about your career. To give it up over what? A difference of opinion? Do you have some personal stake in this?"

"An impersonal one, maybe. At his insistence, we all thought of Parkinson as the disease, but he was only a symptom."

"Do you have a cure, Erica?"

"Sadly, no."

"So, you and your moral imperative are walking out the door," Jamie said. "To where, exactly?"

"I have a ticket to London burning a hole in my pocket. I plan to see Alan's final performance in *Othello*. After that, he'll be back in New York to begin filming on a movie."

"So, it's off into the sunset with Prince Charming. How convenient."

"That's not quite how it works, though it's nice to know that someone else's career is chugging along. I'm leaving Brixton, Jamie, not civilization as we know it. Something will turn up. It may not be the life of the mind, but I'll manage. I hear that bounty hunter is a growth industry."

"Is this all because of Parkinson?"

"No, not *all*. It's just that, knowing what I do, I would find it hard to show up for work. I can't quite summon the indifference I would need to get me through the day."

"You won't stay to fight the good fight?" Jamie asked.

"The good fight is the one I'd stay for," she replied.

He said nothing.

"Actually, I think that Parkinson got the better of the bargain," Erica began. "Academic presses are crawling over each other to publish editions of his collective genius. Scholars are killing themselves trying to make connections between his early and late works. I'd say they've got their work cut out for them. Our own John Crandall is positioning himself as the keeper of the flame. He'll probably spend the rest of his career editing volumes of Parkinson's work."

"At least he'll have a career," said Jamie.

"It seems we are nowhere near exhausting the meaning of the new sadism," said Erica. "Honestly, it's been an education. I wanted to say that, before I go. I'm leaving now."

"So soon?" Jamie asked, his sarcasm curdling the air between them. "You know, Erica," he continued, "you should be grateful to Parkinson. Obviously, you wanted an out, and he gave it to you—Ibsen's Nora, after all. Try not to slam the door on your way out."

"I'm not a door-slammer, Jamie. I never was." Without looking back, Erica walked through the door, then gave it a back-handed pull, "but I could learn."

The door slammed behind her, a heavy rumble growing in volume as it echoed through the halls. Heads popped out of classrooms and offices, everyone with the same question.

"What was that?" asked Letticia, as Erica passed her in the hall.

"I don't know," Erica said. "It's academic, anyway."